ANTHONY
THE IMPRISONED ONE

MLH

RVL Publishing

RVL Publishing

ISBN: 978-1-7339100-0-2

Cover image by Marcel Hawkins

PRINTED IN THE UNITED STATES OF AMERICA

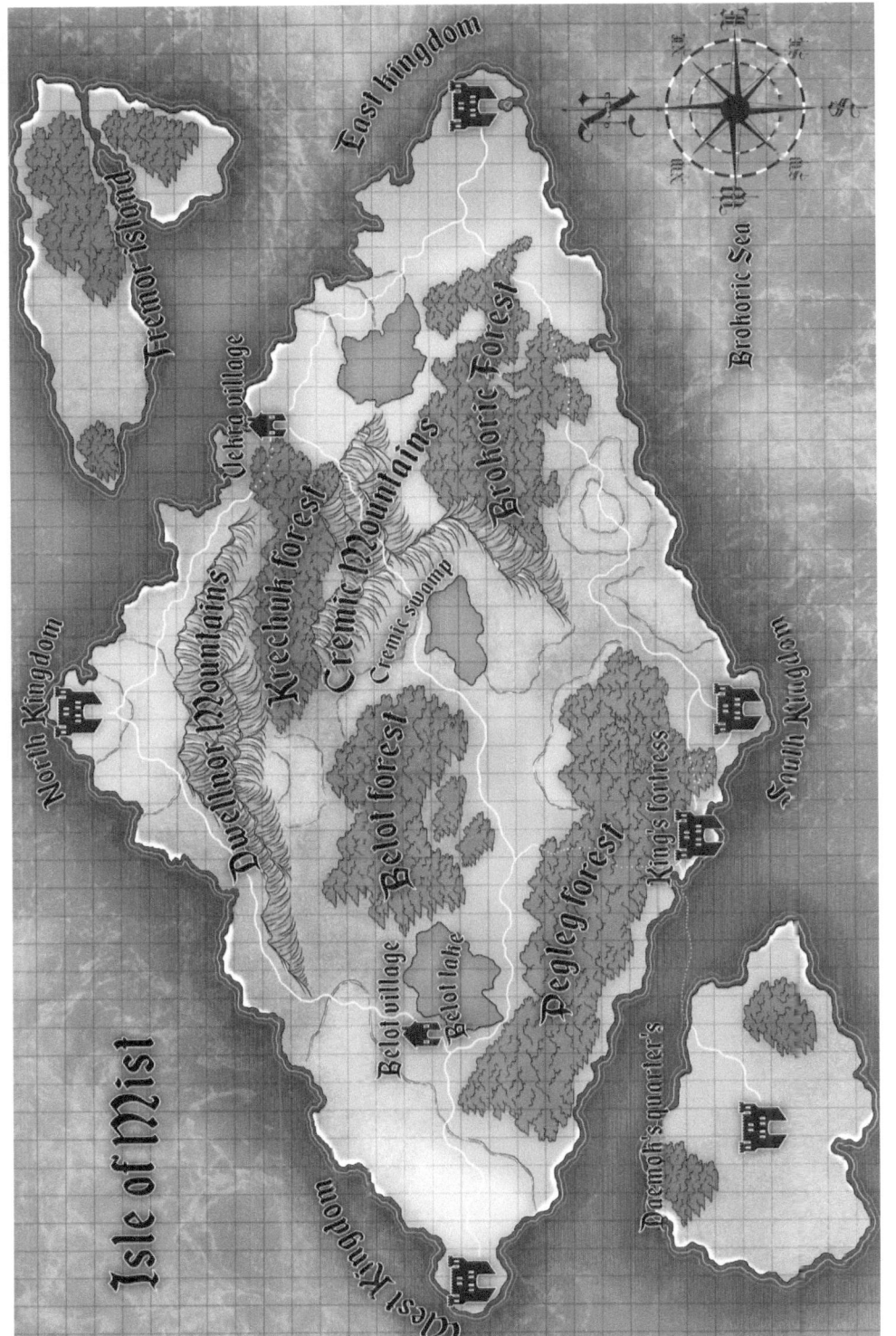

Isle of Mist

North Kingdom

West Kingdom

East kingdom

South Kingdom

Tremor island

Dwelnor Mountains

Krechuk forest

Cremic Mountains

Cremic swamp

Brohoric Forest

Uchia village

Belot forest

Belot village

Belot lake

Pegleg forest

King's fortress

Daemon's quarter's

Brohoric Sea

1

PAST FORGOTTEN

Fire tips caressed the nocturnal sky in a tribal dance. Four sticks laid horizontally over a pile of scabrous rocks with backed trout the size of bowling balls on each end. Two of four sticks were picked up by one skinny green hand with blister sores, while the other was shaggy under clean cut nails. The goblin took half of the fish in one bite. A game of hot fish took place between the Brutar's dentures. His chest armor watched him grab another fish and scoured away. After his, he ate his second. The Brutar attempted to guess how many constellations.

"Stunning, is she not?"

The goblin took his last smack and replied, "Brother Merrick, with you everything is beautiful."

Sir Merrick gave a secret chuckle "Well I suppose it'd be onerous to argue with you, Brother Daemok."

The goblin knight's head steered to a convoy of stars. "It seems to have more of a glow than usual."

"What do you see?" Sir Merrick hummed.

Daemok's squint lassoed another gathering of sight straining lights in the sky. "You first. I'm still looking."

The Brutar took a lungful and shut his eyes midway.

"I see two knights who will map Chaizo into a peaceful era."

The goblin hid his smirk under a miniature frown. He gave a light scratch to his head. "That's the plan, but if we stick together, there is nothing we can't achieve."

The crooks of his mouth watched Sir Merrick turn up and look away from the sky, back at the goblin cased in the same armor. "By the way, congrats on your title of 'Knight.'"

Sir Daemok returned his brother's stare and replied, "Thanks, my brother."

Sir Merrick and Sir Daemok raised their open hands before they clinched like brothers would before battle. The goblin's eyes and body leaned toward the last stick.

"Now let's enjoy the rest of this night with a splendid meal."

The Brutar knight watched as Sir Daemok grabbed the stick, then snapped the last cooked fish in half and stuck it on the tip of the twig. Sir Merrick caught it and raised it in front of Daemok.

The goblin knight did the same thing as the warm breeze swam through them for a minute and proclaimed, "Brothers till the end." Sounds of stars bursting mixed with heavy smacking of warriors conjured a faultless evening. The goblin king swayed his fingers out of the peaceable memory. He sat, a leg over his knee, and with loose eyes crawled up his imperial door.

Giteex swallowed a puff of air in a wispy cough and turned a knob of gold.

"Not even a creek," he whispered as the door opened.

Flames from the red candles lit one side of the room. Giteex's nose flared.

"Cherry."

The rushing wind stole the goblin's eyes at a window up ahead.

He strolled past a large bed mattress beneath sheets that looked like melted gold. His eye embraced the indirect light outside.

Giteex's eyebrows flew toward the breath on the glass.

"Not a slight chill."

His ear canal expanded behind a whipping crack above him. The goblin's nerves went numb as he pulled up. One remained closed while the other caught a bird cage the size of a cloud. A glare from the polished gold attacked his lazy eye.

His sight flexed from the back of his head at the cage swaying back and forth.

"This can't be peachy."

His head deterred from the swinging coop and scanned the room in front of Daemok's bronze desk.

He rushed his head over the lever and spun it to the left. Giteex mumbled just when his hand released the lever. The inside of his palm ran a water park as the cage rattled inches away.

He squinted at the black space lounging outside the column of bars. Giteex wrestled a few steps before his head leaned until his nose sniffled from the touch of the cage bars. Eyes raced side to side.

"I've never seen her around here."

Giteex almost snapped his neck behind his iris with a swift turn. His body froze up in position to a woman. He sized up her rich chocolate skin dusting a few books by her fingertips.

"I take it by the kinkiness; anyone is always new."

Her white gown danced alongside her giggle.

"I presume you're Candis?"

Her senile-assed giggle disappeared.

The goblin knight's eyes cramped as her thumbs paused.

"That was my name; these days I'm not so sure."

Giteex's glance met the silk marble tiles of Daemok's floor, about to inform her why he was summoned before she cut him off with a swift tongue.

"I'm aware; just leave the dress on the chair and get out."

The goblin knight slowly stepped to the chair as his nostrils shriveled to bits from the polished leather stalking the pillow stuffing. He let the dress escape between fingertips like dough onto a baking sheet.

"I'm required to escort you to this evening's supper."

Candis's lips didn't move an inch as her eye caught Giteex moving from the chair out of Daemok's bedchamber.

The purple grape skydived onto his cherry tongue. His posture straightened in front of the chair; edged cut diamonds engraved on the seat spotlighted the meaty feast. Daemok rose from his seat and tucked his gold and crimson doublet, which hugged over his six-pack.

"Sir, we should begin?"

Daemok kept his hands gripped on the doublet before he steered ahead at a feminine voice.

"Certainly."

The smile coiled as the Brutar attended to the bare chalice beside him.

"My lord."

Eyes climbed over the seventeen-foot honey-gold table as his full arms exposed his ripped chest. "Welcome, Sir Usterik, and my apologies for forgetting your name."

The Sifei's eyes enlarged next to the goblin around her clutched arm. Plates, forks rattled above the table from a raucous clap.

"What is it? Ahh, don't tell me; give me a second."

The wine pitcher rumbled in the Brutar's fingertips.

Daemok's fingers snapped "Gabi, my apologies."

He responded with a light bow.

Her head lifted for the two seats from him.

Gabi scowled as her fangs released a discourteous grit.

"Get your futile hands off me!"

Sir Usterik shouted, "Behave!"

She hurled an oversized bundle of spit on his forehead.

He mopped the clotted wetness with an open palm with the other upraised at her face.

"Witch!"

"Usterik!" Daemok yelled.

Her palm grazed her lips before it stopped.

Usterik bawled his fist, mumbled "Witch," and stormed out of the Imperial hall.

"Sorry about his piss-poor presentation of chivalry."

Gabi's eyes bowled the hand fondling her crimson dress.

"I'll add that to the many improvements needed—speaking of which, welcome as the newest edition."

His eyes speared through her tar dress prickled in diamond bits.

The word "ravishing" slipped from his lips.

Her arms swaddled on Giteex's as he escorted her into the seat

---

right next to Daemok.

Candis scanned the table of steamed turkey, chicken and other meats she cared not to pronounce.

Daemok's hand wrapped her palm.

"Savor the feast, my dear; it's delicious."

Candis's focus steered from his hand as Gabi strained her jaw, alongside the fork she held under the table. Her heart hammered her chest as the utensil pulled her hand above the table. Candis's eyes loosened at the Brutar servant slumped inches next to Gabi. She whispered, "The freak," as the fork blades lured from the table toward the kneeling Brutar's eye.

Candis shouted, "Quit it!" at Daemok's grin.

"Anything you'd like to share?" he uttered.

Gabi's bite hardened as the fork's end scuffed the servant's pupil.

She said no with a shallow breath.

Daemok's smile lingered.

"Is there wax in my ears? Because I can't hear a thing."

Giteex's eyes fogged as Daemok's index finger plunged deep inside his ear canal.

Candis squinted as his finger tussled inside a few more seconds before he withdrew it.

"Ah, not a crumb."

Thumb and index rubbed a crisp flick.

"I guess it's not me, so it definitely must be you."

Her honey-brown eyes dimmed red before she yelled: "Alright, no, I have nothing!"

Daemok blew a soft breath and replied, "I appreciate it."

Gabi blew out a ball of relief when the fork fell.

The Sifei massaged her left wrist as the Brutar slave got up and moved back in place through the cricket silence.

Daemok's scowl drowned inside a smirky mouthful.

Candis's eyes fluttered behind bottomless breaths.

She plucked a mauve grape from the plate in front of Candis as the goblin king's chin rested on the top of his left hand.

"If you're seeking refuge or awaiting rescue, let me be the first to announce it'll never come. With that brushed aside, let's dive into business."

He emerged a soft cough.

"The four kingdoms were a spiteful by-the-book organization that needed to be struck down. We'll rebuild power and order in one castle for all to enter."

"As long as we're slaves, right?"

Daemok sneered.

"Is there no better honor?"

"I'm expunging this sullen system and replacing it with a simpler arrangement that seats everyone in their rightful place."

"What you're talking about is dictatorship. Are we not individuals?"

"People have already been robbed of self ever since the royals decided their lives held the highest value."

"You trust your way is the final solution."

Daemok locked his fingers and replied, "No, It's the only answer."

Gabi slammed her hands into the armchair.

"I pray to the seven you die choking sluggishly for this, one day."

Daemok kept a steady grip on his grin.

"Perhaps I will, but for now I'll wait." Her palm sweat poured into the chair arms.

"I've taken notice of how the creatures in the field respond to you, whenever you move their direction. It tells me they back away out of respect or heart-wrenching fear."

Daemok hummed another light cough.

"Judging by your unladylike temper tonight, I'll go with the second. I mean, after all, you're a Sifei; it's what nature called you to be."

A Brutar servant next to Gabi picked an empty chalice up and poured a red substance into it too much like blood.

"No," she whispered.

"I've also taken heed of your blood halt, and you hid it well. Impressive, really, but you made a teeny slip-up."

Gabi's parched eyes moistened.

"Everyone in the Imperial yard still had pulses."

Gabi's eyes turned to glass as her heartbeat conjured a massive thump.

Candis watched the Sifei stare into cherry-colored wine with fumbled lips.

"Since you disagree on my theory that everyone has their strict place, what better than to prove you wrong with a simple test?"

A test? He really is sick.

"In the cup in front of you, soaked halfway, is fresh blood."

You don't have to tell me; I can already smell the virgin pulp tugging my nostrils, Gabi thought.

"So, here's the deal. If you can prove me wrong by not indulging in a drink within a timeframe of two minutes, I'll consider your plan for Chaizo's fate, but if you fail, you must accept your fate, and your purpose is what I say it is."

Gabi closed her eyes. One eye pinched the other.

"Is that even fair?" Candis asked.

Daemok kept his stare on Gabi.

"The wheels of power have tumbled in your hands; what will you do?"

The Sifei's perspiring palm stirred beneath her.

"Come on, you can do this; it's just a little blood. Okay, maybe a lot of blood, but you held out for three months, and this just another day."

A Brutar servant's head dropped when honey-brown eyes faded to a feathered red.

Daemok's cheeks grew defined.

Daemok uttered, "Now the real fun begins," under his breath.

Candis' stomach turned watching Gabi's body create a puddle around her face and chair.

Daemok relaxed her strained legs with an elevated hand.

"I know you're not trying to walk out, because that would be cheating."

Gabi's teeth stirred a crack as she bit harder.

"You let me out of this damn chair."

Her brain took on every muscle.

She closed her eyes and rotated her waist as far as she could, to the left.

Gabi's iris clamped a bit harder as the other one shook away from the chalice's touch.

"This isn't love," she repeated for about a minute and a half.

Coming in on ten seconds, Candis's eyes darted when her helping hand was knocked away as Gabi grabbed the chalice and slurped.

Daemok's lips held a reunion in a slapped smirk.

"Well, looks like the betting god was on my side tonight."

Gabi threw the chalice of wine behind her and pushed on top of the table. Food plates and cake pieces exploded on several faces.

She charged him with fangs out and eyes redder than a ruby gemstone.

"Goblin heathen!"

Gabi's eyes of terror simmered.

Daemok's head tilted left as extended his palm few feet from Gabi's chest.

Her chest dress tangled tornados of air as she flew off the dining table and slid across the marble floor.

A shrill squeak struck ears as a Nairy butler gave her a hand back up on her feet.

"If you insist on behavior not befitting a lady, you will be treated as such."

"Says the man with slaves." Gabi handed him her knotted dress.

The goblin king's head swayed from the reply with snapped fingers; he made direct eye contact with the Nairy butler next to her.

"I believe that's enough play time for today. would you be so kind as to escort her back to her room?"

The Nairy nodded.

Gabi's hand swiped his away.

"Take your hands off me; I can do it myself."

Daemok's smirk settled.

"Then, by all means, please do!"

Gabi's scowl held no bounds before she lifted the ends of her dress and strolled off.

"No, not you, my dear."

Candis's eyes widened.

"I have a pleasant surprise for you."

She watched him rise from the chair with an open hand.

Candis swallowed from her dusty throat and connected her right hand. His raised hand lifted Candis out of her seat. Her dress wiped the floor as Daemok led her to the dead center of the Imperial hall.

His fingers stroked her elbow up to her palm as the other brushed her petite waist. Candis's eyes closed halfway as the pressure Daemok's head nod fiddled melodic music. Her feet followed gracious footsteps all over the hall. Near the doors, his hand raised and twirled her body three times in sudden turns, resting her back on his knee for a quick second.

"For a vile-hearted, pretty-looking goblin, he's a lot better at this than I predicted."

"Not what you were expecting?" he mumbled.

A Brutar butler leaned into another and said, "Kind of reminds me of the king and queen in their glory days."

"Far from it, idiot."

The two let another fifteen minutes skim by before their eyeballs stretched like a slinky.

"Why did they stop?" Giteex asked.

Daemok added more pressure to her midriff as his lips reached for her ear and uttered, "I know who you really are."

The pupils in her iris unveiled themselves.

2

BLIND

Mr. Immel fell back next to an abnormal shaped tree as the shadow of echoes crawled inside a hole within a giant boulder. The Sallus tiptoed in right after. Fingers slid across the goo substance in a slight snarl.

Ten more feet inside, Mr. Immel's eyes squinted in pitch black beside the desolate silence.

"The hell?" he said, to the abrupt floating ball of fire.

The Sallus had turned to another flare, followed by a fire in an accurate ring formation.

His heart dashed down to his feet and back up his chest before his ears rang a loud bell as the circle closed.

Mr. Immel dropped to his knees. A wizard then proceeded to walk next to him with a hand glued to the back of his brainpan. Teeth clenched, as a hand attached itself to his mind. Mr. Immel's growl shook the floor when the witch broke it in seven pieces; the wizard took a bit and passed out during the remaining time.

Mr. Immel fought a hand up.

"What the bleeding hell is going on?"

The Otek grazed the tips with their eyes in the center.

He nodded half a minute later before the Sallus's blood-curdling scream dented a few fractures in the boulder's foundation. Dark-brown eyes shed to jet black in a bundle of flashy memories.

The first several images revealed a towering above a younger one with bruised hands and uncontrolled breathing.

His head let slip two eyes buried deep into another, yelling, "wiseacre Immel, get up after being knocked down."

A female Sallus, with eyelashes curled to her forehead, refused to run away with him.

The witch, heavy in a trance, witnessed a crowd applauding him as he was appointed teacher, shortly after a little boy who always talked during lectures grew into the teenager they were now hunting.

She gasped out of the vision in a wheeze of air before she charged the kneeling Sallus.

"Where is he?"

Mr. Immel's throat muscles tightened as her hand clenched.

"I said tell me!" he squealed like a wet duck.

A wizard stroked the furious witch's shoulders as he nudged it left and right. The fist loosened, as did the magic chokehold over his esophagus. Mr. Immel watched their hands draw back their hoods.

Eyes swayed in pressure in front of seven scarred faces.

"You look surprised."

Mr. Immel rattled out the throbbing migraine with a few shakes and stood on his bare feet, gazing into the eyes of Witch Kadell.

"How fortunate this is; the intruder not only met Hizard but has been teaching him."

Mr. Immel, answered, "Who, Anthony?"

"So that's his name?" the witch disrupted.

"Listen, I know you plan on murdering him. Yeah, he causes trouble; so, does every teenager. It's hardly worth a death sentence."

Witch Kadell paraded next to Mr. Immel and patted his head.

"Silly bear; don't speak on the unfathomable."

Mr. Immel hurled a light growl.

"That said, you will aid us in our endeavor to track him down."

Mr. Immel surveyed the room again—all seven, that time—and blew a cloud of air.

"Well, it's seven against one. I don't have much a choice, do I?"

"You right, you don't." She nodded.

An eye furled for the hoods that flipped over seven heads.

"Hey, lay off!" Mr. Immel yelled at the stable hand around his toned bicep.

"Let's get going!"

"Hold it; wait a damn second," the Sallus shouted before the Otek paused.

"Aren't we going to rest first? This seems like a long journey." The wizard's nails deepened the crease on a crowd of veins lazing on his bicep and continued to stroll out the mountainous boulder.

3

THOUGHTS

Flutters of humming came together in a sugary lullaby as she picked up a silk beetle and sewed a dark-blue shirt. Stitch after stitch, the melody harmonized. Coming in on the last stitch, the smooth hum dropped to a distant groan behind a blurry-faced figure with a tattered red robe.

Anthony's eyes shot open inside a puddle of sweat.

The boy swiped a finger across a string of snot walking toward his lips and plugged another one over his flared nostrils from the pile of the dust as his eyes fixated on the abnormal cage. A clenched punch met the surface of the wall to his right.

"Careful, or you might just end up in here with me, and when you do, I'll decorate this ship with your brain matter."

Anthony left the hostage with a stiff shoulder spin and eyes ahead as he strolled up to the space in the main deck. Arms relaxed on its edge, lips pumped a little air and he peered at the squadron of stars. His breath settled underneath a Brutar constellation.

"Awesome night," Haracle interrupted.

Anthony's head peered up with his eyes cornered at Haracle and he replied, "If you say so."

Haracle reached in his pockets and pulled out his sundial.

"10:00 p.m." He exhaled with closed eyes.

"Finally, the universe is rightfully aligned."

Eyes filched as he told Anthony, "I know this isn't the best."

"What happened to me back there?" Anthony blurted before the Kapos's lips could blur the comment.

Haracle's gaze froze as Anthony's lit up.

A flash of black and yellow inside a red robe struck Haracle's thoughts.

"Anthony."

He soon rammed an open hand ship's frame.

"Don't give me that Anthony crap."

Haracle's head stayed dropped with not a word.

The boy's nails dug into deck's wood while the other hand clutched a beige shirt as he shouted, "Why are you standing there idiot-minded, when I asked you a question?"

Eyelids down and mouth sealed, Anthony uttered, "I said..." before a black hand of smoke tapped his shoulders.

The teen's eyes unfolded as Sir Fowke's head shook.

Anthony's wrist swatted through the ghost's and walked away. He watched the boy parade to the opposite side of the quarter-deck with a careful eye.

Not far left, Arsena's attention deterred away from the fine grind of her daggers.

Anthony threw his body down with mingled arms.

Should I say something? she thought.

A buff breeze of wind hushed her a few seconds until gentle grind snatched her focus back.

The boy's head tilted against a massive piece of wood before he exhaled and closed his eyes. Forearms rested on a kneecap as his fingers twitched to the sound of his voice.

Frantic pats with an open hand on his knee joints caught his attention as he analyzed up the Importees.

"This the hundredth I've tried."

"Lost count after eighty," Benevlo responded.

"Pull a hundred to a thousand and get back to work."

Anthony forced himself up from his knees to his waist and wobbled to the enormous hole in the tree.

14

"Come on, you can do this. Remember, control is key. If you must, we can take a break."

The boy's hard breathing was cut off in a second with a firm fist.

"You're mistaken; it's agreed this training has no doubt more bloodshed than any I've experienced. A real challenge always makes it hard to contain my excitement."

Benevlo's eyes fired open as the boy dived in the hole.

He watched as the Importees stitched itself together with Anthony inside.

The crimson troll's eyes shut within absolute silence and counted down from twenty seconds.

Nineteen to fifteen seconds and nothing... turned fifteen to ten seconds.

Ten seconds flipped to five seconds.

"Come on, kid," Benevlo uttered with a lowered head.

A blinding light ripped the Importees' stitches. The troll kept a hand over his face as the tree spat out a figure.

On his stomach, Benevlo smiled as the boy blew out a ball of lit-up dandelions.

"Like I said, excitement!" he said, before he his head hit pillow of grass.

The troll's smirk faded as the Importees patched the hole completely closed.

Irritated waves pulled the boy's mind out of the Importees and back on the clipper. His hand opened and shut four times before a rude thump shook the whole boat. Anthony's eyes beat his body from the floor as his pal Haracle flew to his side.

"What the fenkel was that?"

Anthony steered around and up to the main deck with his sights lunged at the large transparent clipping mask torn to bits above the main and quarter deck.

The ship of sapwood was painted with cannon holes.

"Bazooka holes, probably," Arsena uttered next to the boy.

The boy's eyes rolled.

"Like I already wasn't thinking that."

Anthony pushed away from Arsena and back down the quarter deck.

Benevlo shouted "Wait!" as the boy pushed off on foot into a huge leap onto the other ship.

Anthony fought his dancing legs on the deck's weak foundation.

Arsena shadow dashed next to the boy.

"What are you doing here?"

"Shhh, trying to get away from you."

The Pessamanti growled in his direction as he kept its eyes tweaked for the main deck with words.

"Plug it, mutt."

"Are you ever nice?" Arsena commented.

Haracle flew with a gust of wind and behind the two.

"Quiet!"

Anthony's head turned and he replied, "When did you get?"

Haracle laid a hand over his mouth before he could finish the word here. "I said, quiet, dumbass."

The rim of her lips curved as his eyebrows tangled, "I'll give you a dumbass."

She rested her hand on his shoulder and muttered, "Seriously, settle down."

"So, you can it hear too?"

Arsena nodded as the boy's eyes opened and stood still as the Kapos tiptoed forward before a sharp creak tore away the eerie silence, followed by two more.

Anthony's body shifted for the faded paint door grating open and shut before his heart began pumping blood throughout unfamiliar veins.

In door's reach, he grazed it by the end as eyes lunged pitch-black space, on the other side.

His head stuck out like a giraffe as he stirred a complicated glance.

"What could be behind the black door?"

A mattress of wizard's fire encompassing the boy's feet shoved him left in a flash as the web-shaped ice sickle charged his right eye.

***

Anthony's eyes trailed the web toward the back of Haracle's head. He ran for it with hand out.

"Haracle, watch out!'

The Kapos began to spin to the obnoxious scream as his eyelids pried the tip to a knifed web kissing the back of his skull.

Anthony's eyes widened as the web fell into the jaws of Arsena's pet. She watched it hack it down a couple of times before the creature let out a baked cough.

Anthony's slung his focus back on to the huge area with a hand up engulfed in fire.

Another kit of silence brushed the boy's ears as his eyes stayed forward.

"Anthony!" He turned to the long pitch of the Kapos's whelp.

The brown in his iris crinkled as he whispered, "Why in the seven is Haracle playing with a stick?" He continued to watch him tussle with the rust-colored stick in front of his face while the corner of his other eye caught a flying bat emerging from the black space.

"Oh, damn!" he yelled as a bunch of upside pyramid teeth came for his left eye.

Reflex threw him in a backward roll with a streak of fire meant for the hovering stick of death. The boy's gaze loosened when the fire gutted the creature pie.

"The freak!"

Anthony's rushed to Haracle's side and yanked the stick off his forehead with a fire blast.

"What the hell were those?"

Anthony finished watching the stick sizzle to ash.

"I was hoping you would tell me."

Haracle's mouth remained shut with eyes front and center for a second until the Sifei's curb stomp intervened.

Anthony slow walked behind Haracle as he jetted to Arsena's side.

"You alright?" he asked.

Arsena flicked a bit a tad bit of guts from her boot with a solid shake.

"Sickening," she spat out.

Anthony gawked a nod before returning to Haracle's chalked eyes.

"What's up with you?"

The Kapos's finger aimed for the black hole behind the door.

Anthony's nose flared as the blackish space swelled.

"Move!" she called before a swarm of paper-thin creations with dozens of legs opened for their faces.

Anthony ducked as Arsena dashed to the side before Haracle 's wings scooped him up a centimeter above the speared webbing.

Anthony's hands, coated in wizard's fire, impeded twelve of the critters with only three blazing streaks, his smirk short lived as another set spat his direction.

The boy's knees bent and twirled his body into a flawless 360 as the web of ice sickles shot past him.

"Oh no!" he whispered, back on his feet with eyes jetted for Sir Fowke's sailboat.

Benevlo squinted before he wailed, "Watch out!" to the sprinting web.

The Brutar ghost's eyes dimmed as he disappeared in a large net of smoke.

The crimson troll's knees sagged with his head down as eleven hit the main deck's granite floors before the last one struck through intricate wood on the quarter-deck. The troll in the cell peered its pale eyes at the ceiling to the floor in a second.

He stared at the gash on his shackle lock with a big smirk.

Arsena nibbled the bottom of her lip as a couple more of the creatures sought to remove her legs from her waist.

She scurried to the left as her sword sliced through several racing webs. Her eyes edged her panther of smoke feasting with an ashy mouthful.

She smiled in a slight head bow.

"Look!" Breaking her sneer, Anthony kept a hand doused in wizard's fire and the other pointed at hundreds of beings crawling back into the obsidian space.

Teeth stayed clenched as his foot pounced through the rotten wood.

"Come on, don't get scared now!" he commented.

Haracle slapped a hand against the boy's chest.

Anthony exhaled cloucs.

"Damn--what the hell, Haracle!" The Kapos's eyes stayed forward as the boy's other hand extinguished next to his still eyes.

Arsena squinted as a few couples scrambled a hill inside the squeaky door. Haracle's fur twitched when it sealed. The boy's puzzled look wouldn't leave as Arsena imitated his stare along the canvas of the main deck. Haracle's ears wiggled as his heartbeat played like a stereo through obelisk quiet. Still, like reference sculptures, his eyes exploded like a puffer fish as a sudden flash carried the three off the galleon and inside the ocean's throat.

4

LOCATION

Sets of supernatural hooves bullied the angelic blades of grass. Sayno's smirk lit up his green eyes of mist as he sank in the thought of royal citizens' screams flooding his ears as their dissolved lungs released a plaguing cough before they spat out pepper orange particles. The wizard's horse kept a controlled pace on top of the same color, conjuring a path through Pegleg forest. When his lips curled and the scent of baked candy cane attacked his nostrils, he whispered: "Just a mile further."

Coming up on a hill, the horse paused.

Sayno hopped off and took ten steps forward and stopped. His right hand raised in front of the giant area of air occupied by three tall trees. He touched the wall in tiny circles.

The concentrated frown flipped as the diamond brick blinded his mind with a smile growing every second. He shadow ported back on his horse, riding it around and out of the forest.

A few shields of magic within the diamond brink, fairies snoozed on chubby clouds as the vibrations of spoons clamping bowls with crystals engraved into cups stomped above a twenty-foot dining table.

General Ino let go one of the turkey legs cleaned to the bone on a plate beside him before he let out a stomach-aching burp.

"So, what's the plan of action?"

"If weren't stuffing your beak, I'm sure you could have come up with something by now."

The hippogriff scolded the snake as he picked up another leg of meat and chomped away.

"Give me a few minutes' mouthful."

General Byron signed and looked to the dragon tranced by four thrones. He coiled next to him with a swift slither.

"Seems like yesterday we were drinking to one another's success."

"Except one thing," General Ton responded.

Eyebrows ran to his nose.

"I don't drink."

General Ton traded a smile with the general of serpents.

"It's beyond understandable why they wouldn't take a seat."

General Ton hummed.

"My generals," Sir Canshu uttered with a bow.

The two generals eyed the Brutar knight in a head dip.

"I'm fully aware of the undisputable situation our hands have been dealt, but I'd like to offer a tangible solution."

"Tangible?" General Byron chuckled.

General Ton leaned toward the Brutar Knight and said, "You remind me of myself when I was a knight. One thing I had never learned that I had to was boundaries, and this topic is one of them."

Sir Canshu's heart throbbed with moist palms.

"My apologies," he responded with another bow.

General Ton drew his head back and watched the Brutar strut out of the Imperial Hall.

His ears perked the gallons of water underneath the fortress bridge.

Halfway off, Sir Canshu's ears ran toward a lullaby that led to a sunflower garden.

He smiled. "Figure you'd be here."

Her song eased as Sir Canshu took a seat on a bench across from the Brutar queen. Sir Canshu laid a hand on top of his knee, as she uttered: "Can I tell you something? Well, a story, honestly."

Her fingers danced inside a sunflower bed.

"A tale of a little girl whose father passed from an incurable illness. She prayed to the seven for change every night and weeks before his death. But the bucket of miracles remained emptier than her words. She stalked the walls of his office endlessly. Her mother was a stone writer for the castle at a time when such a skill wasn't in abundance. Well, on her account, at least, until one night she saw her daughter having a field day in her sunflower garden she had planted. At the time, it seemed she tended to her flowers more than to her daughter. She rushed to her garden and wrapped her daughter like a python as she told her she loved her to death. She didn't ask her to stop or why, because secretly she had to have known--instead, she dug a small hole and handed her four seeds and watched her pour them in.

"Add a little water,' she instructed before she hugged her daughter once more in what was the best night of sleep she ever had. Sun woke her from the hearty rest. The Brutar princess rose in a sky-sucking yawn.

"Her eyes hopped for a teen sunflower blooming in the midst of her sight as her mother woke not long after. She removed the flower from the ground and put it in her daughter's hand. The girl twirled it the petals by its stem and believed faith was the lesson her mother taught her that day."

Sir Canshu kept a hand over his mouth.

"You should know I've told this story to only one other person."

The knight breathed.

"No coincidence the Brutar king would request a sunflower garden planted in the King's Fortress."

She smiled then frowned in the course of five seconds.

"Suppose not."

He broke a sunflower from the bundle of twenty and dropped it into the queen's half-opened hand as he lifted her chin with an index finger.

"We will win this fight, take justice back, and as long as air fills my lungs, that's what I fight for."

Her pout was freed. "Thank you."

Leftover soot and wind drove their tarnished helmets and chest

armor off Dwellnor cliff. Seven steps up and forward scattered plen-
tiful bird beasts with four eyes instead of two, plucking bags of dust.

The goblin king passed through dust heaps in front a big boulder he once called prison before a black flash flung behind him
faster than he could turn. Circle, side to side, coming left, Daemok's
head sunk with a smile as his right hand stuck out for the monster's
throat.

"Impressive. I didn't believe you guys stalked the world
anymore."

Daemok noosed his clench as the shadow bounced up and
down.

"Pacify down; I have a grave task for you." The jerking froze. The
goblin king kept his lips straight. "That's what I thought."

5

UNCHARTED

Fingernails bled deep near the top of the cliff. Reznark's teeth couldn't have gripped harder as his biceps and triceps worked together to haul him up the cliff. The holes in his drab green cape fluttered as he stood topside. He looked down the sky cliff and rubbed lips in a smack before he honked a ball of spit.

He blew a whistle of relief as the spitball disappeared somewhere in the clouds, turned away from the sun, and peeped through the ample space with scattered unlit torches and tents made of Dyra skin.

"It could have much worse, but still," he muttered as he climbed down in the occupied space. He couldn't make out whether it was a village or camp as he roamed through the filled area. Decomposed blood forced its way into his nostrils. He plugged his nose with one finger and walked past the put-out fire.

"Couldn't have been more than thirty minutes ago."

Near a tent, a silhouette like him but a little taller froze behind him. Reznark 's throat tightened as his left hand clutched a hatchet before his stomach touched his ribs and flew ten feet back.

The goblin knight pushed himself up back on his feet and scowled at two goblins thumping his way with fists cocked back. He wiped the blood off his chin and threw the hatchet in his hand on the bloodied floor.

"Alright, you want to play, then by all means," he muttered and stepped back in a quick dash with an arm locked against the first goblin's neck, before he rammed his body into the stony ground. His waist twisted faster than the second goblin as he shot a solid kick to his saggy gut; he immediately bent over as Reznark's palms held onto his ears before he gave the tribal one a steel knuckle to the jaw. He watched the force from the punch sent him crashing to the ground. He stared them down, one on their back and the other on their belly.

"Don't tell me this what the goblin king sent me down here for," Reznark commented before a hatchet guard cracked the back of his head. Eyes rolled in a thin number after his toned abs landed one of the tapped-out goblins.

The Shadow near Reznark stood with blood dripping from the cut on his head and exhaled through a Dyra skull.

Minutes flipped to hours after the sun descended above the bed of fire. Mr. Immel's right hand slept under his chin before it flopped and glanced right to a mix of wizards and witches sleeping inside their shadows. His eyes returned to the swirling flames.

"It is still hard to grasp that about a month ago I was teaching a student, and today I am helping to hunt one." He peered left with his eyes before they lunged for the green insects crawling toward a flotilla of leaves. "So, this is the Brokoric Forest." He stood up and tiptoed away from the fire and the Otek for the forest. "I must see if Anthony is in there before they do."

6

DISCOVERY

F lashes of water and bubbles attacked his unconscious brain to a special night. A pair of nine-year-old hands clicked rocks and blew thick air of frustration as the spark disappeared before his breath hit it.

"Damn!" he shouted before he gave it another try. Click, scratch—on the third click, the first turned in his grip and scratched the meatiest part of his palm.

"Dammit," he wailed. He threw the other into the Crofik forest and watched the trees consume it.

He shot his left hand in front of the fire and let out a settle fire streak on the pile of sticks. The eyes of the monster hidden in the bush's hurried open as wizard fire trickled from the boy's fingertips.

"That's what the talk is all about," he said, before his ears perked to crisp leaves rustling another.

Anthony's hand sprinted for the bush.

"Who the hell's there? Show yourself!" he commanded, with fingertips of fire aimed at the shrub. "Have it your way," he yelled before a flutter swelled as big as the creature that dashed out. The boy's eyes creased his forehead before his classmate flew off. Anthony ran a few seconds after, although the animal had a head start.

Anthony's breathing declined the deeper he jogged into the Crofik, until his eyes caught the Kapos in plain sight. Trickles of fire from his simmering soles shouted "Gotcha!" before he threw his body with his arms and hands out.

He grazed the Kapos's hair on his back as his wing fluttered with the help of gushing wind. Anthony's eyes popped as Haracle thrust far forward before he slipped into the jumble of bushes. He spewed a mouthful of dirt and a silhouette.

"Please, you can't tell anyone!"

Water filled his lungs into a giant cough as his eyes opened at the call of his name. He glanced through pitch-black surrounding and looped a few enchanted yellow rings shining around them.

"Figure you'd be the last one up," Haracle commented.

Anthony's eyes scattered.

"Where the hell are, we?" he uttered, away from the glowing rings toward the sudden slit in the bubble. Arsena's eyebrows clapped for the shadows through the Kapos's eye studying the amphibian-like creatures that stood on two legs, while Anthony gaped the significant cuts across their necks.

"Gills," he assumed.

Arsena's pupils enlarged in front of a small fin that laid with pride above their cherry-red eyeballs. The boy's nose swelled as they directed a large enchanted ring against their nose.

It's not much different from the rings encircling us, he thought.

"Get up; she wishes to speak with you."

Haracle snapped his observation behind and thought, these must be Fhimels. *Never* sparked my interest much, but standing front and center, I'd have to say my eyes can't look away.

The boy's hand rested on his knees, and he pushed himself up.

"Who the hell might she be?" he asked.

The Fhimel's long-drawn fingers encircled their arms and threw them in and front out of the bubbled entrance.

"Easy, man," Haracle uttered as the creature rammed his hip.

"Move it."

Anthony's fist stayed hardened as they followed a Fhimel in the front and the one in the back with a ring pressed on Haracle's spine.

A tad cold, he thought.

Arsena's arms folded as her eyes wondered out of the stretched bubble. Her lips reached for four gigantic more bubbles with jillions of shabby stone structures inside.

Fifteen feet down, the Fhimel stopped for a second before it tucked the ring by its hip and moved aside. Haracle's head tilted to the right as his eyes laddered down the black abyss below.

"How the hell are we not inside that right now?"

Arsena's foot poked his heel.

The Kapos's head wheeled and gave the Sifei an eyeful. What? he thought.

Arsena raised her chin ahead. Anthony's fist unclenched with paused breaths. A foot-long floor with a gap inside, to Haracle's eyes, added sparkles to the crystal pond within it, below bright green lily pads.

Anthony sniffed to the voice, "Stop!"

Arsena peeked over a pile of water, conjuring a large chair. The boy's shoulders stiffened as the apple-red cape slid around the chair. Anthony cupped around his neck as the creature changed its direction. They studied hundreds Fhimel kneeling, seconds later, before the Fhimel tucked her bum against the chair. Anthony took the sight of the abnormal shark fin more massive than the rest swimming up her head and down her neck. She took a gentle seat. The boy's chin itched before the Fhimel floated alongside. He wondered why she didn't fall straight through the chair of water.

Arsena's lips fought the irresistible to bite her nails as silence took the room. Haracle cackled at the four great white sharks swimming behind her. She resisted with a chewed tongue as he flexed his temple as the Fhimel's set of teeth separated.

"Long hail Udar Kimmie."

The floor rumbled as hundreds of Fhimels recited.

Anthony's shoulders slumped as the room quietened some more. Fifty years ago, this place was nothing but free ocean; that was until leader Udar and his bride Kimmie.

Anthony's eye fidgeted toward two whopping bare-fleshed Fhimel statues standing outside a bubble she stood beside.

He thought, they turned this place into something unimaginable.

"As you probably noticed."

The room beat itself dead.

"What?" Haracle uttered.

The Fhimel strolled out of the chair onto the Waterous floor.

"A wizard draped in black sought a special book we kept, and in exchange for it he promised to heal the unusual sickness our leader caught wind of."

The Fhimel lady coughed.

"With the wizard agreeing to terms, he began going to work; unfortunately, he wasn't harboring a cure but a spell."

"What kind of spell?"

The Fhimel lady paused for eight seconds.

"Streco xi mo."

Arsena's eyes raced out her sockets.

"That spell was made as a last resort to erase Chaizo if Hizards happen to take over."

The Fhimel nodded.

"But the wizard was somehow able to conjure it on a small scale."

"How are you still standing?" Arsena asked.

Her eyes went to the floor of bubbles. "I was furious that my sister was forced to be his bride, so I gathered hundreds of my followers and swam away to venture off for a colony of my own. That was before I caught wind of an immense blast several miles away. Weeks later, I--" Tears shoved her eyes before she waved an incoming Fhimel guard strolling her direction. "We swam back with sore fins, not to the aftermath but a graveyard."

The boy's forehead narrowed.

"The violin solo of this story is amazing, but what does any of that have to do with your men snatching us down here?"

The Fhimel lady's tongue stood still again for a few seconds before she replied, "I suppose you have a point."

"What was the wizard's name?" Arsena interrupted.

The boy's mouth lapped upwards.

"Is that significant? Deep down, we already know who it was."

The Sifei tugged her eye nerves forward.

"That's great for you, but I'd still like to know for sure," Arsena replied.

The Fhimel's tears dried on her cheeks.

"No one knew him, as he never shared his face underneath his hood."

She exhaled and thought, nothing is that easy, before the Fhimel inside the apple cape strolled nearly face to face with Anthony.

The boy's pupils expanded as she studied him from head to toe.

"I've never seen a human—a strange one indeed."

"We believe," Anthony shook away in a gross cough.

"Water, quick!" she demanded.

He hacked again. "Water? That's funny, but I'm fine."

Anthony watched the Fhimel step away from him and back in her chair. "I've had my men summon you here because we may acquire your help."

"With what?" the Kapos uttered.

She jolted upright.

Anthony cut in, "Look, whatever you are I don't know and won't ask, but we've got our own set of problems."

"Don't be a rude ass," Arsena blurted.

"An ass who is stating facts."

The Fhimel's arm rammed against her chair.

"Listen, human, or else you'll be thrown back into your cell."

The Fhimel guard's rose to the boy's nipped tight fist.

"Do what you have to, but there's someone out there important to me, so unless you're offering your assistance with her return and to seal my empty vengeance, every other word out your mouth is potted feces."

The Fhimel lady stayed still for five minutes.

"Escort them back to the prison."

Hands still tied around his back, he said, "That's fine. I'll be out, when and when I am, I'll gladly take you as my first kill."

Haracle's head sunk next to Arsena. She watched the Fhimel

lady give Anthony a once- over as his back disappeared down the thirty-foot hallway.

Four hours back into their cell, Arsena, Haracle, and the boy sat in zero noise.

"You're so stubborn," he uttered.

"Guys, this may not be best area or time for this."

"You mind repeating that?" Anthony uttered.

Haracle chomped down as his feet pushed his body up. "You heard me. You're freaking stubborn; all the meagre lady wanted was our help right now."

"The same lady who is holding us against our will in this pitiful excuse for prison architecture."

Anthony exhaled.

"Besides, what do you care, as long as you get fed? Your whiny outrage isn't directed at me but at the unwavering feast that wasn't welcomed."

Haracle glared in the boy's vacant brown eyes. "Curse you!" he said, before he turned away. "Back at you; we've got our own issues."

"An understatement, for you," Haracle puffed.

The slit in the bubble flung her mouth open as the Fhimel with a red cape strolled through.

"Have you considered my proposal?"

Haracle wheeled into her direct line of sight.

"I'd be honored to."

She nodded thank you.

The Sifei got up next. "Count me in under one condition."

They gave each other their eyes.

"Sure, anything."

"I'd like my pet back."

Her forehead wrinkled before she answered, "Oh, that blasphe-my beast of smoke."

"Exactly that beast."

"Hideous," she commented.

Arsena took a light step forward.

"Your opinion is your own, but I'd still want him returned."

The Fhimel lady's eyes ran a circle.

"Fine, you may have your pet back." She proceeded to look at Anthony. "Should I bother to ask?"

His middle finger popped between her eyes.

"Expected no less," she uttered

"Alright, we shall be off," she announced with a mild clap.

"Wait," Haracle disrupted.

Lady Fhimel's tar-black eyes shined at the Kapos.

"What do we call you, besides Lady Fhimel?"

"Yeah, what is your name?" Arsena mumbled.

Lady Fhimel's glare froze at the two for half a minute.

"Not of importance."

Arsena and Haracle watched her drag her cape out of the cell bubble. She followed ten seconds later as Haracle rested at the entrance with Anthony still sitting in the ridge of his eye. There was not a letter of exchange as the Kapos flapped out of the cell. He kept his attention at the white scuff on his black shoes before he ducked his head as the cut in the bubble closed.

"Idiots," he whispered.

Almost at the bubbled hall, Arsena mumbled, "Should we really be doing this without him?"

He leaned in. "Not my brightest idea, but his head is in a different place right now. Trust me, he's better off in there, as are we."

Arsena's eyes sprawled from Haracle in a secret. "Like you can do no wrong."

"Alright, straight to it." The Fhimel lady clapped.

The two teens' glares dissolved and steered toward a gush of water shooting from the floor about four feet.

The Sifei's eyes couldn't break free from the pancaked puddle conjuring at the top as Haracle's eyes bulged toward the center of rushing water shaped into a pillar with the Fhimel lady's face spiraling around it.

She pointed to an open spot on the flat puddle.

"We are here." She slid her fingers six inches to the left. "According to my intel, Captain Fluko should be here."

Haracle squinted.

"What makes your intel sources so sure?" he questioned.

The Fhimel lady smirked. "Because, know-it-all, that's when she wakes."

Arsena's eyebrows fluttered in thought. *Saying it doesn't sound good would be a cliché, but I still must know.*

The Fhimel lady watched the two eye what wakes without saying it. She spun a few feet from the smooshed puddle and secured her eyes in front of the two statues.

"I've seen many creatures in these seas but never heard of a rugged beast so vicious and bloodthirsty as the Annihilator."

Lips zipped and sanded eyebrows darkened over the two teens.

"Rumored to be born in the darkest pit of the abyss, the creature's mother killed its father moments before its birth. Her mother passed seconds after her birth. Left to fend for itself, the beast scoured the abyss, observing, learning but dangerously so—adapting."

The tips of his eyebrows kissed.

"Others believe it's about to awaken from its three-year sleep, but personally, I'm certain it never sleeps and is only risen."

"I presume it's coming to the surface, not out fun but necessity."

Their open mouths stirred drier than a toaster oven.

"If you're asking yourself if I've seen it, I have never been that lucky." She untied her back and strolled up back up to its mouth. "For some reason, this year it decides to feed, way ahead of the usual cycle."

Their heads followed her finger in an open area of glowing blue on the map.

"Massive amounts of aura and light tremors have been quaking the black seas."

"If it's the creature, why rise early?"

"Low on food, possibly," Arsena commented. The whites of her eyes grew dry. "I'd bet my life on Captain Fluko being there, front row."

The Kapos took a step toward The Fhimel. "Why would he be anywhere near there?"

The corners of her lips grazed her cheeks. The Fhimel lady's hand-knotted again as her cloak paraded past the two and stopped in front of the statues again. Eyes heavy concentrated outside bubbled glass.

"Whatever it is, we'll see it the early sun."

The comforting hum broke through her lips as he entered. She bristled her curly hair with three fingers within the gold-plated cage. She continued to tune out the song without words.

"What's the name?" cut a fine string through her halted fingers.

"Excuse me," she answered.

The goblin king drew two steps toward her.

"Don't," she immediately blurted.

Daemok froze faster than his body and nodded off course. Stillness somersaulted between them.

"Just wanted the name of the lovely tune playing from your sumptuous lips."

Fingers slipped away.

"A futile man like yourself wouldn't understand."

Daemok grinned and replied, "Come on; I'm itching for it."

Candis's lips remained vacuum-sealed.

Daemok's smile simmered. "No need; I'll know about it very soon."

You're insane, she thought.

He clapped and stepped four steps away from Candis before he wandered her direction once more. "Make sure you're in your rightful sleeping position before I get back."

Candis's frown dove in a scowl as Daemok walked out of his room. "Bastard," Candis muttered underneath the visceral slam of the door.

Awakened stars stood over snoozing sky. Mr. Immel dug a neat footprint between a city of branches below. His eyes folded toward a fleet of trolls gathering around a tree. The Sallus's arm rested under his jawbone.

"I wonder," he uttered.

Seconds rushed to minutes as his ears perked to the continuous line of melodic voices. His paw consumed in soot, he lifted the other one forward. Eyes hopped back with pulsating pupils underneath a sharp sting in the back of his head before his lumpish body of fur fell into the arms of two Otek members. Half an hour imposed as the fireplace from whence he sat fluttered in small blurs. He rubbed the small bump dancing on his head as his back stood up.

"What happened?"

He glanced again in ovals and saw the exact stick he used to trace over the spiral. His gaze went full course and stopped in front of five sets of robes. The Sallus's brow puckered in detail.

"Why did you bring me back?"

"Can't have you doing anything flat brained, like warn the enemy."

Mr. Immel sat stiller than he already was. "You expect me to sit by while I watch you hunt and hack down a fifteen-year-old boy?"

A wizard grabbed a long stick next to the Sallus's glossy claws on his feet.

"I wouldn't expect nor want you to."

His close-fitting eyebrows relaxed.

Wizard Pai sniffed an air full.

"We're all where we need to be--past, future, love, and hate doesn't matter. Because a person can have all these things and end up where they thought they'd never be."

The wizard's blemished face left the statement inside a simple breeze.

Mr. Immel's arms crisscrossed.

"Why's that?"

Wizard Pai's hand stopped waving the stick in the earth's grime and stared Mr. Immel in his sunflower petalled eyes and replied. "Circumstance."

His strong brow untied itself.

"Remember that," the wizard demanded as he got up and walked over to the fur-stiff Sallus's side and placed a withered hand on his collarbone.

"You don't have to like it, but fast or slow, it catches up."

Mr. Immel gave his hand a light shrug before the wizard took it off.

The teacher's eyes drowned out the wizard's voice, informing him he would aid them to catch perhaps his most important student.

Beneath night's darkest hour, Sayno galloped through a stew of bleached smoke. His eyes leafed past stockpiles of stone ruins. Fur hooves halted on top of a pancaked stone. The wizard hopped off his horse and stooped on the flat rock with a few fingers funneled over a triangle inside a circle. The creature eight feet away glanced as the wizard paraded through another fence of black mist. The goblin king's eyeballs faded from absolute black to lightened red. His fingers twiddled with his index fingers alongside the cottony tempo of his feet.

"What are you up to?" slipped from his lips before he fired out of his shiny seat. Daemok's footsteps hauled for his bedchambers. He gave the doorknob a tender twist. The diamonds on his turban matched the heartbeat of his candle dancing on his table as he strolled to the wrinkle-free sheets on his bed before his head laddered toward the cage capped in sheer gold.

A puny sneer broke free as he watched Candis's chocolate skin complementing the cage of gold as she snored soundlessly before he proceeded back to the silly gold mattress underneath cardinal blankets.

7

VOYAGE

The sun's yawn bullied the night's sky as chunks of water spiraled beneath the ketch's blades. Veins in the Fhimel's neck ticked back and forth as their arms and legs freestyled closer. The flicker in the Kapos's eyes twitched when the water's current blackened.

"We're coming in closer, soldier!"

Arsena's palm painted her necks as the honey in her copper-colored eyes went red as the army of Fhimel's floated a foot under Captain's Fluko's eroded ship blades.

One side of Haracle's eyes peeped the overheated red consuming hers.

"You alright?" he asked.

"Quiet; it's almost time," the Fhimel lady whispered.

The only thing weirder than breathing underwater is having conversation beneath it as well, the Kapos thought.

The Sifei's lips stayed fastened and ears flared a vast of alloy hooks dove shy of ten feet from his sights, accompanied by mad ripples onto the water's surface. The Kapos's head shot up at the call.

"Come on, wussies—more anchor throwing and sweeping, and less groaning!"

Far left, a ship apart, Benevlo uttered, "That's not odd."

Sir Fowke mocked his eye direction and peeked toward

twenty animated buff skeletons marching with more bones than a churchyard.

The troll's eyes struggled to break side to side from the god, and shaded rag hugged their shaved skulls.

Arsena looked up and asked, "What are you waiting for?"

Haracle and Lady Fhimel's eyes tightened another set of bronze hooks anchored below them.

"Now!" swelled out her throat.

Captain Fluko expanded a mountain of water splashes, while the he jerked the crowd of shadows descending from the sky onto crying wood. Body of bone flexed as Lady Fhimel paraded from the back of her militia to the front. Lady and captain, shipmates and soldier's eyes flexed their jaws.

Benevlo's breath hastened as Captain Fluko's lips untangled. "Slay them all."

The Fhimel lady's tongue tossed the words back at him.

Sir Fowke watched a pillow of seawater ripple beneath the ship as Fhimel and skeleton charged for one another. The captain's left hand reached over the tear in his jacket pocket and pulled out a ball of gas shaped like brass knuckles. He observed Arsena's daggers swinging right and left through pins of his men next to a strange jaundiced-looking glow cutting through several more. Haracle watched the captain's lips unmask his teeth before he welcomed several Fhimels to the end of his knuckles.

The brim of lips tugged into a grin as the Fhimel blood fed the dry deck. His feet of bone stroked through the blood a few steps away from the burdensome panting singing from the Fhimel lady's jaws.

Haracle's chops remained closed, like he had no lungs, as his bone and flesh skipped over his head.

The crevice of his right iris latched on to the skeleton sprinting for him. Haracle's bladder would've drenched his legs if he hadn't leaked it already. The buff piece of bone with a hammered fist raised just as fast the Kapos's head lowered. His eyelids shielded the abrupt explosion of bone raining on his face as the last streak of it slid off his shoulder.

"Odd time to dreaming of me," Arsena commented.

"Thank you" wavered from his lips as the Sifei bled her grip on her daggers and aimed for two more rampaging her way. The sprinkle of red from her eye twinkled in a flare as a stripe of fire sliced through their chest and neck. Haracle nudged his eyes back in place as the glare from the sparks revealed the boy's face.

Anthony's comment floated with the thought *girls* as he glanced at the turgid curls in her air before they fixated on the yellow fungus baked on a couple of his spilt toenails. The second wave of disruption cooked his hands with pits of ember as another gob of sprinting skeletons headed their way.

The brim of her lips went underneath her cheekbones and replied, "I was wondering when you and common sense were going to schedule a date."

Anthony's chin jutted.

"How'd you weasel your pitiful self out of the cell?" she asked.

"I'll let your curiosity handle that one," the boy replied.

She shook her head and said, "No, you'll tell me after we deal with these Bonys."

The order she attempted to give the boy flew past the boy's train of thought with the question, What the troublesome is a Bony?

Arsena watched five more circle his feet before his legs threw him forward with arms tucked apart from his waist before he leaped into a dog pile of animated bones.

The Kapos kept his selfish stare on his feet as the Sifei pranced her glare away from the boy toward the Fhimel lady strutting the end of her cape within range of the captain.

The ship's captain veered his hollow black sockets at the Fhimel lady's delectable black eyeballs.

"Looks like you stopped hiding."

She smirked and replied, "I've been taking this thing called bravery out for a whirl. He chuckled back. "Idiocrasies of bravery, please do tell."

"Doesn't make senses to waste any more breath on what a skull beast like you would claw his eyes out trying to comprehend."

Captain Fluko shoved his fingers into his palm with a slight fist.

"Well, it appears you already did that. "A tunnel of air was swallowed by his heavy jab before the left side of her cheekbones gave in to the wind-slashing haymaker. Captain Fluko's grin was uncontainable as she released a bowling ball of blood from her mouth, capable of knocking a strike.

Captain Fluko paced forward and followed it up with another splitting haymaker to the face before the left side of her cheek caught another hug from his fist. She made a strident turn to the right and introduced the base of her left foot to his backside of bones.

The bottom end of his feet grew sultry as they carried him six feet away. The Fhimel lady used the top end of her right hand as a napkin before they charged one another again so fast that the blood sinking from her lips couldn't even hit the floor.

Their heels slung at one another like a slingshot.

"Just die already!" the captain of bone roared.

Teeth lubricated in gore, she hurled, "That's my line!"

Some feet across the ocean's bed, the fog on Benevlo's glasses intensified as the dim on Sir Fowke's red eye became darker.

"How long should we let this carry on?" Benevlo asked.

"When it happens, you'll know," the Brutar ghost replied.

The tip of Benevlo's tongue was interrupted by an ill-mannered shadow port from Sir Fowke to the front of the main deck as very back of the blazing beam of the Lunis went straight through the ship's main floor.

Sir Fowke observed Benevlo take off his glasses and smudge any residual fog with his index finger, before he lifted a fist toward the battle-ridden galleon across from them and yelled, "You want me to write you all prescriptions, so you can see when the fight is getting away from your boat?"

Sir Fowke took a baby breath and commented, "Maybe we should fix our prescription so you can see its pointless yelling at a group who is more than fifty feet away."

The crimson troll held an exposed hand to his near his visage of smoke and said, "Shut it."

Benevlo observed the four wood-ridden holes and advised, "I'd better tend to those."

The Brutar ghost gave half a smile and clarified, "Not if you plan on turning this boat into a soggy submarine, I approve of the repairs."

He resumed his stares as Benevlo strutted for the holes camping at the end of the main deck with his right hand surfed more purple than the color itself. Sir Fowke's neck shifted his head back toward the battle fifty feet from him and he whispered, "Come on, kid."

The party of bubbles from a troll they kept prisoner slid by his focus as the brigade captain paddled his arms in the water toward the Lunis light show on the other ship.

Burnt to crispy cutters, a set of healthy nails above beige- shaded fingers clawed its way up and onto the ship before he pressed his hands on the ship's bound and vaulted over it. The troll's white eyes grew whiter as it scanned through the clashing fists and Lunis. His glare enhanced as the boy's figure arose through a pack of smoke.

He shrieked a mouthful before hot pent up air traveled up his lungs out his mouth in a shout. "Human!"

He examined Anthony disintegrating a heaping helping of Bonys before his free hand bawled with his feet sanded into the creaked wood before he dashed through bundles of bones. Their parts flipped and scattered through the air like prize confetti as he continued his dart.

A few feet away the throbbing vibration from his thumps tenderized the boy's feet.

He socked a Bony in the face and raced his fist for the top of his forehead. Fire tugging his feet landed him to the side and six feet from the troll's hand of death. Anthony 's widened eyes stretched.

Not to be on the opposite end of this question--how did he escape? he thought, seconds before Captain Abornell spun his body left into the perfect windstorm with a mallet fist. Anthony ducked, and with his right leg gorged in wizard flames, he swept for the troll's drumstick calves.

The troll captain hopped above the leg of fire and darted for the teen with an open hand as soon as he landed. Anthony's entire topside pinned inward like a foam ball as the troll with the milky eyes gift wrapped his face with his fingers before his back rammed into Captain Fluko's doors.

"Imbecile, stop! I do not have a quarrel with you."

Captain Abornell's murderous scowl sharpened.

"Then that makes you an idiot, because the only way I'll ever stop is death."

Anthony's heartbeat went irregular as the troll's grip imprinted his skull on the door. Feet soaked in wizard's fire, Anthony drove his knees into the troll's bulky chest before Captain Abornell's hands hugged away the flames dancing on his abs.

He backed away for ten seconds and dashed for the boy again with an elbow out and pinned it against the teen's Adam's apple.

Anthony's arms and feet fluttered.

The troll's nose flared in a smirk. "I'm feeling better already," the troll commented. When Anthony rose, the constant kicks and neck wrestling came to an uneven halt.

Captain Abornell's eyes lessened their whites as the boy's eyes expanded behind him. The troll's grip weakened as his head turned like a steering wheel.

Hundreds of spit glassed eyeballs the size of clouds was staring Anthony and the troll down. Every nerve on the ship slayed in time.

"What in all things seven...?" Captain Abornell whispered before the beast with a multitude of eyes shrieked buckets of drool onto everyone on the ship. The troll let go of Anthony, and as he veins thawed, he separated the tip of his elbow from the boy's swallow tube and darted for the ship's border.

Anthony remained paused alongside everyone else.

Captain Abornell put a hand on the ship's end, and with a leg already up, before his jittery eyes relaxed one of his ankles within the muscled slime substance. His attention couldn't hustle any faster behind him.

A cup overfull with a stare flooded his face before the tentacle making love to his foot scathed for his calf and yanked it back like a vicious thief. Anthony's breathing calmed as Captain Abornell hung upside down by his left leg. Haracle's gaze knew no bounds.

"This must be the infamous Annihilator," he presumed.

An unseen spark flew in Captain Fluko's vacant eye sockets as he uttered, "It's more beautiful than the legend."

The Pessamnti whimpered behind the Sifei's coat as she locked on the beast lowering the urinary-trembled troll in her mouth. Captain Abornell puffed "Curse your gut," before an uncountable set of teeth began reeling the gap. Eleven tips from its knifed teeth filleted a shredded bit of skin from the troll's scalp before a ball of swollen light pierced a couple of the beast's irises. Anthony's arms and legs were smothered in wizard's fire. The creature dropped the weighty troll after it reeked a few more balls of fire to her eye. Anthony slung his arms over his waist in a 360-degree spin with a shot of fire from his feet. He stuck one arm out in mid-air while the seared one clamped onto his shoulder blades and shouted, "Fire Ryder," before a cloud of fire floated beneath his feet carrying him away from the creature and back toward Captain Fluko's ship.

Anthony looked down and uttered "of course" as the fire cloud began going on and off broken shutters.

"Come on, not yet.

The drenched Fire Ryder sailed eight feet from the ship before it dissolved within the night's winds. Anthony jerked his legs up and down in wizard's fire and, dispatched in a seven-foot roll, grabbed Captain Abornell with his hands and slung him back on the ship before himself. The boy tumbled nine feet like a coin before his rib-cage tapped against the troll's leg. He shoved it off and crawled over to the boy and gave his cheek a knuckle feast before he stood up.

"I don't recall asking for your assistance."

The teen smudged the pain stinging on one side and murmured, "Chrome dome bastard."

Captain Fluko and the Fhimel lady watched as the Annihilator slumped back into the water and submerged the last eleven

---

43

tentacles. Every sowed mouth on the ship heeded the theme of chilled bubbles fiddling the veins of the wind.

Anthony launched himself up from one knee and the quarter deck's edge and glimpsed over and squinted for the heaps of waves trampling one against the anchor's home. Four Fhimels poked their heads, not a minute after Anthony witnessed bursting bubbles cut itself off. Silence finally won the round as they glared at the still waters much before four tentacles too much like an octopus rocketed out of the water and attached themselves around the three nosey Fhimel heads. The Fhimel lady screamed "No," before it dragged them into the famished belly of the ocean. Captain Fluko's grin latched itself to the Fhimel lady's frown. The passionate wind spilt her radical red cape as she ran for the confines of the quarter deck.

Her footsteps backed away faster than his hands shook fire. He watched as the remaining goodly sized tentacles surfaced before they began to sink into the sea mattress.

Anthony's legs reeled for the two octopus-like suckers transporting the rest back home. Anthony scolded the last parched eye drowning itself. His own eyes wagged back and forth at the crashing waves cleaning whatever trace was left by the vile creature. Anthony tilted one end of his mouth as a fist bumped the other end of his mouth. The boy's eyeballs spiraled sideways as his bottom palms broke his fall in a roll. The boy stood on one knee up at the troll who stood with his feet spread apart with a fanning fist.

The captain smirked at the red veins in his eyes taking over.

"There you go," he uttered.

"Enough; I'm ending this right here!" the boy mumbled.

Haracle's chest pumped out rapid breaths as halls of terror lounged in his stomach. Baked eyes were Captain Abornell's in his stomach. Cooked with fury, the troll was refrigerated by a sharp fling of his head forward into the invisible brick wall. The troll's vision went blurry above his quivering knees. Arsena owl-stared as the troll raised a knuckled hand partially before the entire front end of his torso tore another hole onto the floor. A small breath mingled with her words before the beast emerged with gallons of water skydiving from every inch of its flesh.

Captain Fluko commanded his shipmates not to move a centimeter, while the Fhimel lady ordered the remainder of her troops to steady their weapons for the creature's eyes.

Arsena caressed the daggers from her sheath beside Haracle's sculptured stance. Not a single flinch stepped out of line before the beast forced its jaws apart in a lumber-shattering roar.

Everyone rushed their hands over their ears after the creature's geezer shut. Anthony took a brash step forward with a knotted fist as his eyes greased to the end of their sockets.

The beast's chin and the roof of his lip divorced in another vicious screech. It became a race to see who could shield their ears the quickest as hordes of wood from the captain's ship ripped off and through the abdomens of three Fhimels and Bonys.

Captain Abornell 's goggle sent thirty Fhimels soaring off the boat into treacherous tentacles. Anthony counted to eight before his heel compelled his body forth in a killer sprint. The beige troll faced him with his arms spread out, revealing his bosom of aos. Anthony's eyelids stressed his attention as he affirmed, "We're far from finished."

The fallen brigade captain's forelimbs clutched one another as soon as Anthony knocked his to the side.

"Human scum, you're mine." Anthony transferred wizard fire from his hands to his feet for an extra boost before he launched through Captain Abornell's tugged knitted arms in a massive front flip onto two of the beast's tentacles. The Annihilator's heart stuttered as he separated two of her tentacles holding the boy's legs above it.

"You can do better than that," the boy shouted with his weight leaked to his knees. Haracle's awareness secured the teen's feet, tossing him in a backflip. Anthony's irises glistened; his arms raked through the sky as his heel stomp dampened the pulse on the beast's head.

"Watch your back," Arsena howled to the sudden fatty Annihilator's wabbly swing.

Anthony lobbed his body to the side as the group of tentacles that were once behind him positioned themselves front row.

In the Sifei's head, she wailed the boy's name until she lost count as her lips stayed glued, before the stray tentacles struck his lumbar region. The troll entertained his gaze as Anthony flew toward the ship like a flying saucer. Captain Fluko's head followed his body, smashing through another door on the main deck.

Dust and wood piled on his lap before he coughed six times. He kept the ripped portions of timber on his waist as he got up. The moisture from his tongue was entombed in airborne soot as he beaded his eyes for a pair of jars sweltering two headless beings. A tiger with one gigantic eye in the middle before his eye steered away for the tangled bunch of ugliness stored in the second jar.

"Creepy room for a creepy captain," he mumbled.

With a hand playing in wizard's fire, his head jeered an urgent turn at the words.

"Get him, men--don't let him escape."

Anthony lurked at the head on display once more and said, "Excuse me," before the wizard's fire propelled his dragging feet and body like a bazooka out of the hovel he had entered.

During his side flip, the left end of his ribs clashed against the troll's dukes. The heat of the blow was air conditioned by heinous circulation of wind, tossing the boy's body into the marine of the saltwater.

The pit within the ocean devoured him before the prickle from his ankle made its way throughout his mocha flesh in a swarm of eel-sized piranhas. Inside the yarn of bubbles, a motion picture branded itself into Anthony's psyche. A demonic entity took up the form of a shadow behind a woman in white gown with its fingers laced around her throat. Anthony kept an eye on his seven-year-old self, frowning upon the wicked presence whipping its unpleasant tongue over her cheek.

"Help me," she pleaded as the cracked door near them began to lock. Anthony continued to stalk his younger self, sprinting for the door, more out breath with each step.

The painful slam braked his pants before the teen's buckled eyes shook open underwater. They flickered a laser lemon yellow three times before they burnt brighter than a tangerine. A jet stream of bubbles imposed from the boy's mouth in a prodigious roar as seven branchlike spikes sprouted from his spine. He paddled his arms into big circles. Coming within the ocean's lid, the huge rings his forearms waved lessened as the bottom of his quenched their coldness with a chunk of wizard's fire to his toes in a crowded blast and hurled his right arm, pitching a massive blade of grassy green fire.

Captain Fluko screamed "No," as the gliding disc of ember sliced through twenty of the Annihilator's tentacles, easily.

The words "Hizard fire" mumbled from the smoky tips of the Brutar's ghost lips. It was impossible for Arsena's eyelids to go any wider for the tornado of water snuggled around his calves. Captain Fluko's hairless eyebrows curved as the boy hovered his stare for the sea beast squawking its way back into the singing sea.

Captain Fluko gritted the cover and bottom end of his toothless orifice and spat out a plate of spit.

"Attack!" spilt the concrete inside of his ears.

Anthony's orange iris steered toward the seventeen Bonys pulling and pointing their swords for the airborne teen.

Anthony outstretched his right hand and levitated every Bony from the ship above the pit of water, except the captain. The teen concealed his smirk before the Bonys crumbled to ash with the clench of his right hand. He lobbed another orb of forest-green blaze for the connection of bone holding Captain Fluko's feet together. If he had eyeballs, they must've fallen out before he leaped over the ship's dock and dove into the water seasoned with his comraces' ashes. The boy watched the captain for nine seconds more before a cocoa brown ate the fluorescent fire orange in his eyes.

The whirlwind heaved beneath him and evaporated into a boiling panel of steam trailing a sweltering storm. Arsena continued to gawk as Anthony plummeted through the gob of powder ike smoke seconds before he imprinted his back on the stone surface of the ocean.

Benevlo said, "I don't know how much more I can take." He turned ahead for the crimson troll and inhaled a room-sized puff of air with his eyes closed and replied, "It was becoming vexing anyway."

The velvet troll gave a mild caution as Sir Fowke disbanded into a veil of smoke from one to another. Haracle's jaw dripped as the Brutar ghost put an arm above the shiniest spot on his bald head and chanted "Conco."

The Kapos lurked as the snow white in the troll's eyes darkened before his whole frame tumbled backward as if his nerves and muscles had clotted.

Sir Fowke latched the other hand on the unconscious troll and vanished into another clog of smolder. The Fhimel's neutral grip around their Lunis strengthened as their stare struck the Brutar ghost reappearing behind the Fhimel lady. Their weapons uplifted faster than they could blink as he put a misty arm around her neck before he dissipated. Benevlo scanned his hand over the final patch where a prosper hole lingered. The orchid-colored shine exuding from his crimson hand returned inside the pores of his hands as Sir Fowke appeared inches from the preserved hole.

"Dial down the smoke during the grand entrance?" he inquired before he saw The Fhimel lady cuffed in the Brutar knight. He stood up and asked, "What is she doing here?"

Arsena stitched the silence as he grabbed Haracle around his woolly stomach and shadow dashed from Captain Fluko's impaired ship and back onto their own, twenty-five feet shy of the meeting. The Kapos squinted as the Brutar ghost prodded in front of the Fhimel lady and told her, "It would be in your brain's best interest if you spill the location of the treasure."

"A little extreme," Benevlo commented.

He turned ahead at the strutting troll and replied, "I'm surprised a book worm doesn't know when he is searching for—well, you know, a book,"

"I'm stunned you know what a book is, let alone are able to say the word."

Sir Fowke's jaw strained side to side.

The black tongue swirled in the desert dryness of her mouth as Benevlo removed his glasses from his head. Sir Fowke's rosy eyes continued to lurk at Benevlo, using his palm to wipe away the grease streak lagging on his right lens. He locked the temple tips of his glasses on the lanky outside of his ears.

"Better, by the—what's your name?" he mumbled.

The Fhimel lady gave him a faint sniff and said, "Raheria."

"Anyway, I apologize for the sudden atomization, but I would appreciate it if you tell us whatever it is my ill-mannered comrade here is searching for."

Her lips remained quiet as if welded shut.

The interrogation traveled yards into the ocean and tweaked the boy's ears. Anthony's arms followed the movement of his feet like a fast-moving racket. His bag of flesh straightened like a sword-fish as he kept his freestyle strokes for the seaplane.

Haracle's cornered ears picked up the sound of a massive bubble erupting below the ocean. Bursting through the seas like a coordinated rocket, Anthony's eyelid publicized his eyeballs as he ruptured through the bubble of quiet with the base of his shoe touching down on the durable deck of wood.

A peak of water from the eruption showered the boy's already drenched scalp and clothes even further. He looked ahead at his two friends and squinted at Sir Fowke yelling, "Tell us."

Arsena and Haracle's eyes tied in on the three like a cinematic masterpiece, and squeaks coming from Anthony's shoes went past their ears. Benevlo's listeners wouldn't allow him to ignore the screeching ring as the boy arrived.

"You finally done swimming?" Benevlo joked.

Anthony 's feet and body moved past the comedic troll and put him face to face with Raheria. The middle four fingers on his left hand folded around the collar of her red cape.

"What in all seven did you send us into?"

The Fhimel lady said no more than she had minutes ago.

Anthony's fingers clenched a hole in the cloth around her neck. "Answer me!"

"It's useless, more so than her," Sir Fowke uttered.

Anthony lowered his head for eight seconds before he shut it back up and spoke with an echoed voice.

Raheria's heart performed squats in her chest as the teen's iris went from sugar brown to sun yellow. He looked Sir Fowke dead core in his red eyes and said, "You're probably right, and so it appears maybe it's time we stop."

Raheria felt a piercing itch at the bottom of her stomach as if she were being ingested from within. Anthony removed his grip from her cape and watched as she held her front end like she was trying to keep her internal organs from leaking out.

The spirit in the boy forced his lips into a smile as she grunted in a way that would have made a howler monkey proud. Anthony elevated his left hand near her head and replied, "You're going to have speak up."

Sir Fowke examined as the teen's hand burned in a jacket of Hizard fire. The Fhimel lady flew a hand from her tummy to her windpipe. His smirk was stuffed as the muscles in her lungs began tearing apart at his will. She gasped in a struggle as each breath she fought for abandoned her body. Anthony waited until she could puff nothing before his ears perked to the hum of words from her last whiffs.

Arsena's caramel eyes gleamed as the lime fire shock wrapped the boy's left hand and died out. He leaned in with his ear hugged tight near her lips. In half of a voice, she informed him, "You'll find it where everything is found while all is lost."

Anthony anchored his ear from the crust embracing her muzzle and gunned his right hand for her throat in a fearsome clench. The glow in Anthony's eyes rivaled the brightest star as he shouted, "You think this is a game?"

Benevlo ran behind Anthony with his right hiked and spelled, "Kre nuko sealu."

A mild sphere from the crimson troll's palm knocked his head forward. The precipitous blur in his vision faded the yellow from his eyes. The fallen knight continued to gawk at the teen sitting on one knee with a hand brushing his head.

"Damn, let's not do that again."

He analyzed the void ahead and flinched as she ducked from her feet to her back. The boy kept a close eye on Raheria's legs squirming away from him toward the rim of the boat. "Keep away from me!" she begged as she stood up.

Anthony took a step onward before yelling, "Wait!"

The words left his lips just as fast as Raheria chucked a hand on the deck's boundary and hopped over the board separating her from the sea. The melody her body played as she smacked the water's surface pulled Anthony out his trance.

"That wasn't random at all," he whispered.The teen wheeled as quick as Benevlo patted his shoulder.

"Hey, mature man, everything functioning right."

Anthony stalked the crimson troll's left shine just as red as his skin. He sat his right hand within the glow for a couple of seconds before he lured it away. If Anthony had to describe it, it was like he was peeling off a screen protector. Sir Fowke's wagon- red eyes rolled ahead as Benevlo placed his other hand near Anthony's face.

"Hey!" the boy squalled as the carmine-colored plasma latched itself from his cheeks to his forehead. Benevlo laid the other sheet of energy on his face before his eyesight went from clear to raven black. Inside the alarming space, the troll trundled his head as de from his trivial breaths as he searched for any refuge of light.

"Even the wind is pacified," he mumbled.

He scratched the firmness of his hand until it went raw.

The same second, a set of blazing orange eyes stabbed his back. The troll rushed his legs away from those soul-snatchers for eyes. Benevlo's glasses cracked on the end as the bare thickness of his fell into the clutches of a butchering grip.

The hand of death drew him closer until he was compelled to confront the futile optic source of light. Benevlo's heartbeat revved like an engine as his exhales lessened before the skin-ripping rumble came from a mystery figure gazing him down. The big-gunned screech smashed the black emptiness and Benevlo back into his head.

Sir Fowke moved his hooves of smoldering back as the rays of red energy from his and Anthony's faces shivered off like a pottery mask. Anthony watched the remaining parts fade into the salty air.

"What happened?" he asked.

The glare strip on Benevlo's glasses smothered his entire lens as he backed away from the boy. An awkward stroke of hushes stained the air before the Brutar ghost wiped it away with a series of words.

"We're never going to solve that ridiculous excuse of a riddle by standing here gazing into each other's eyes."

Anthony kept his center on the crimson troll walking up to the front of the ship's bow spring and responded, "I'm not going to fight on you that."

The boy's head steered left and right and questioned the whereabouts of the vicious Captain Abornell. Sir Fowke smirked and demanded the teen not worry; he'd been attended to accordingly. Anthony's eyelids closed fairly.

"I'm not afraid to ask what that means."

The Brutar ghost of smoke told him to lower his blood pressure; he was just taking a much-needed nap.

The boy gave Sir Fowke a stiff wave and asked, "Anyway, can we go?"

The two passed one another unpleasant stares.

"Yeah, let's," Sir Fowke uttered as shadow ported the highest point of the ship and yanked the string strangling topsail. Anthony observed as the large sheet didn't falter like a ruffled blanket before he circulated his attention for Haracle and Arsena.

The two stared at him to no end as the ship continued through the sludgy mucus of the ocean.

8

TRUE

A mound of bucketed ash swam through an ocean of pimples. "Sunset's wussy is finally waking up. Reznark hacked remaining gut chunks dangling from his chin."

"I hope the little nap I laid you in wasn't too short."

Reznark's forehead furrowed as his hands yanked back to the chains clamped around his wrist.

"Just enough sleep to rip your throat out and stuff inside your kidneys."

The goblin's smile cowered behind his lips.

Reznark, his back against a chained boulder, let out another spitball as his eyebrows waggled before a goblin. He stepped aside next to the goblin, not much taller, hiding behind a skull mask.

"And who the hell you might be?"

The goblin beside him lunged forward with a deadly punch center in the cheek. Reznark swished six times before he hacked blood on the goblin's feet like mouthwash. The creature with the mask of bones raised a hand to his side and paused the goblin's fist near Reznark's chops.

"Chulko."

His teeth clicked as hands drew to the hip.

A brain-dead name is putting mildly, he thought. His pupils flared as the goblin's hand cupped the skull before he sunk it by his waist. Eyes showered at the size of those bear claws across his face. Unrecognizable, he believed.

He swallowed blank air and said, "Solid makeover."

The goblin next to him grasped his fist and demanded he show respect from the depths of his throat.

He raised another hand, walked toward the chained goblin, and kneeled. "Where are you from?"

The goblin knight eyed the bridge of his burnt nose. "Where do you think? But you probably know him as Daemok."

His eyes synced with his before he shot up. "Daemok is free? Impossible."

Reznark broke into a smile.

"Why so shocked? A true king always finds a way."

The goblin with the skull in his hand turned and replied, "You do well to control your tainted breath about things you have no understanding of."

Eyes swiveled. "Sounds like a desperate sore loser."

The goblin threw his Dyra skull to the dirt and raced face to face.

"Infectious imbecilic, Daemok is the sore loser and coward who left his people to pursue a life with the Brutars."

"I'd advise you to act out some respect," the goblin with chains suggested with bright yellows behind his dusky brown dentures.

"You want to talk about respect, then Samunite is your goblin."

Reznark bit his tongue. "A psychopath is exactly accurate."

"Daemok wouldn't be the scum's scum on my foot if it wasn't for him; hell, he'd be unable to use magic if he didn't steal his research."

"Unworthy to be called his son," Chulko expressed.

"And you're the better choice?" The goblin next to him stomped with his fist cocked.

"Disobey me again, and the crows will have their overdue treat." He enforced eye to eye with Reznark.

The hand held behind him rushed back at his hip.

"Yes, tribe Sukril."

Reznark uttered, "Never heard of it."

His hand drew back. "Not to worry; you will soon enough."

The goblin's eyes reached out burnt skin plastered on his back.

"For now, what is the real reason you stormed into my village uninvited?"

Reznark released hot air.

"Yours? As far as I'm concerned, everything in Chaizo is now the property of Daemok, and I was sent here to convince you to join, but I doubt the goblin king would even consider it, not in this lifetime but any."

Tribe Sukril sneered and said, "Is jokes all you're good for?"

Reznark's eyebrows knotted. "Unchain me, and I'll show what've I've got."

"Oh, you're not even a pawn in this game."

He watched the leader pick his mask from the ground and in his ears and muttered: "Prepare him."

The tent draped in Dyra cloth drowned the continuous fist pounded against bone as Chulko headed inside.

9

REDIRECTION

Jaw bricks wasted away in ample black ash just as the wizard's finger bones crackled at the castle bridge as the hooves of his horse dashed past dozens of royals hammering bundles of granite. He got off a horse and sauntered into the Imperial hall past open-mouthed snake pillars and curtseyed onto a humungous golden plate. The malicious wizard saw his reflection from the healthy waxed circle.

"Rise," the banished one commanded.

Sayno stood and forced the dusky goblin to sit on his shady king chair with a foot in and one out as if he intended to trip someone. Sayno's green eyes glistened toward the micro metallic plates his master played with between his fingertips.

"My lord, I've discovered the discreet location of the king's fortress."

The blunt tips of the goblin king's snappers curled into a smile.

"Discreet seemed overrated for you."

Sayno remained speechless as he continued to fiddle with those halo-shaped plates in a globe formation.

Daemok rewarded the sleepless wizard with a single word: "Excellent."

"Should we prepare to for infiltration?" Daemok raised a hand in front of the wizard and demanded.

"Not yet."

Sayno put a hand over his tunnel of blackness not a foot below his eyes. The middle of his index finger restrained the slippery trinket's motion.

"If the queens indeed still draw breath, then we will continue letting them live in their misery and strike when they genuinely believe there's an ounce of hope for rescue."

Sayno instructed the hand near his mouth toward Daemok.

"Excuse my reluctance, but wouldn't we want to attack now while they're weak in spirit and numbers?"

Daemok's smile straightened as he rose from his throne walked behind it and up to the theater screen sized window. The wizard's emerald eyes grew a shade as they watched the goblin king creep through the sterile glass.

"That's exactly where don't want them to be," he uttered with his right hand up.

Sayno nodded seconds before his black robe whisked him away in speedy shadow port.

Daemok lured his eyes down the bridge of granite as Sayno's sprinted through.

He watched as the horse carried the wizard until he disappeared into a line of trees.

Fifty miles under the burning marshmallow sunset, his charcoal robe flapped as his horse piggybacked him through a tier of sky-scraping mass of molded stone.

Sayno observed the smaller ones and concluded they were nothing short of gigantic. The slit in his cloak narrowed up ahead at even larger grate of stone centered into the ground. He shadow-dashed off his horse right in front of the ancient chunk of rock.

Sayno lifted his arm. "Easy, Rai."

He stood up a second and rolled his baggy sleeve and stuck his right hand out.

"Suku ek noot." He spelled before crashed his hand into the potted earth.

He veered his head to the sky like an old lever before his mouth let out a subtle hum.

Seven beryl glares in the shape of jars climbed from musty grounds onto the spiral carved grave. The wizard pulled his sparkling hand out of the doughy soil. He took a step toward the floating vases.

"Suku ek veal."

His and Rai's eyes casted an impenetrable stare as they crunched to the gleaming scrap near the unattended crease on the left end of his robe. He dragged his sluggish cloak onto the mildewed rock. Sayno's smile leaped new bounds as the seven strings of ash poured from the busted vase. He observed the waterfall of ash pile up dirt like a dump truck. Lump after lump they formed and grew a robe like the shaman who conjured them but without the pitiless green eyes.

Seven ashen-eyed wizards pointed their gaze for one standing in front of them. Sayno lifted a hand no more than a foot from their soulless bodies and chanted, "Suku ek chase." He snapped an arm and finger past Rai.

The seven summoned wizards tricked themselves into their wobbly robes and disappeared. Sayno stood next to Rai and said, "Now, on to more pressing concerns." The spiral that once sat proud in its roots was snatched into couched soil as Rai galloped out of the ruin of stones.

10

REGRETS

Strings of blood plastered the rocky walls, trees, and her dark pores. Her back-chilling laughter could have been heard worlds away as she kept digging, slashing her way inside and through blocks of Sifeis. Her giggles continued as the entrails of men, women, and children hung from their stomachs like Christmas tree ornaments. The creek innards carted her red robe within a grody mirror of blood dancing on the glass like heat waves. Candis arose from the cryptic dream inside the cage laced in dripping gold from top to bottom of her head.

"Nightmare!"

Candis jumped from the figure's shadow brushing the bars.

"Do you care?"

Daemok stood from the rim of his bed toward the dangling cage.

"I don't recall reaching the speaking phase of our relationship."

She responded with bleak silence.

He took another step forward.

"Contrary to what you believe, my intent is not genocide."

She leaned her head and blurted, "No, you just want to control what everyone does, says, and how they do it."

"Beasts living in a crime-infested world struggle to know who to trust."

Candis steered her head at the bunch of softness racked underneath her behind.

"Answer me this: what's worse, a creature who thinks they know their purpose and fails miserably, or one who is given one and thrives beyond imagination?"

The sooty-pigmented goblin's feet moved his top half from the enclosure. The boy's mother swiveled her focus to the gold stripe painted on the back of his cloak. Daemok's left hand skimmed the four bolts holding the door together and replied, "When you have an answer, I'll be more than glad to entertain it."

Candis gave his backside a light growl as he exited the room.

Miles stacked on top of miles from his headquarters as the youthful, cookie-sweet smell of the Pegleg forest matured.

Inside the pyramid of brick, Sir Canshu made his evening stroll over the fortress bridge. The sturdiness of his hooves stooped toward another clutter of Brutar feet stomping his direction.

Sir Canshu hopped side to side as the stampede of generals raced toward the exit. The Brutar knight's eyebrows flared before his legs lugged him their direction in a thick bottle of wind.

"Excuse me," braked their wings and scales. Several feet from the exit, they escorted their attention at the voice behind.

"Explain now," the snake general Byron blurted.

"What's going on?"

The enormous serpent coiled like wavy string and told the Brutar knight to know his place.

"Easy," brother Byron the dragon advised.

He moved some feet in front of Sir Canshu and ordered him to look after the queens while they were out. Brother Byron caught the scent of the king's aura.

The Brutar's lips withdrew above his viscid abdominal plate.

"We have to take a chance while it's still fresh."

Sir Canshu's head tilted at the ray of light coming from the brick under his hooves.

"Isn't it slightly unexpected for the king's aura and scent to just pop up out of nowhere, especially when we're all desperate to find them?"

General Byron reeled his tail closer to his torso.

"Are you questioning my abilities?"

Sir Canshu's hands scraped the air up like a hostage. He said, "Excuse my inquiries, and I say this with the highest respect." Their lightning-fast breaths was caught as he uttered, "I believe it is a trap, and I'm carefully advising you not to leave." They glared at one another. The general's inflexible muscles faced the Brutar knight's gaze.

"Your concern is valid, but sadly, this is not one of those times, understand?"

The rush of words ready to leap from his mouth wasted into a knot of sweat from his palms. He bowed his head.

"Understood," he excused himself.

General Secktor expanded the space between himself and the Brutar knight as the mountainous snake released his tined attention and slithered away and through the gate. Sir Canshu hawk-eyed as the dragon's armor sounded like juddered change as he shadowed General Ino.

"I've got an overly bad feeling," Sir Canshu breathed as the last set of fifty bricks unveiling the hideout sealed off.

11

SOARING

If he leaned any further, he'd fall into the ocean, as the base of his left hand moved back and forth over the shore like a penknife spreading butter. The pace of air walking up and down his lungs stopped as Wizard Palik's fingertips pulled from the small area of water. The wizard stood and shook his hand and stared across the Brokoric sea.

"The Hizard is across here."

"Get ready."

Mr. Immel snorted in secret.

"I've must've skipped the chapter in my books where it stated that wishful thinking was one of your abilities."

The back of his right shoulder was patted forward as Witch Kadell moved past him with her elbows to her arms over the carpets of water and spelled, "Co nik ubble."

Mr. Immel's posture stiffened by the rapid blinking toward seven monstrous gray bubbles. The yellow tint in his eyes molded a trace of light for another encircled portion of air of space more prominent than the others. The left of Wizard Palik's grazed the patch of fur on the Sallus's ankle.

"I'd say I have this wishful thinking on lock."

The brim right side of his lips tugged his left end in a discreet sneer.

"If you don't mind, we can't get in front; we're behind."

Wizard Palik directed his hand toward the darkest bubble in front of them. He watched as the female witch stepped within her hanging bubble above the coats of water. The left and right bottom of his grizzly-haired feet moved in. Wintery and wet pasted to his mind like a post-it notes. Wizard Palik inspected the Sallus's eyes widen as his toes scrape against each other.

Glaring below his feet as he stayed within the transparent breeze ball, he mumbled, "Amazing."

The Otek lead wafted a hand near the rug of fur stitched to his scalp and said, "Conco."

Mr. Immel's eyebrows dropped over his eyeballs faster than collapsing weight. He lurked as his body belly flopped onto the basal of the bubble. His peepers relished in another goggle at his napping body laid flat out beside him like a serving tray. He spared a gaze for the female witch soaring in an iron-colored bubble next to him.

Wizard Palik nodded as the word "Pusho," slipped out. His attention sauntered away from the witch as his bubble moved ahead like a slingshot launched it. Thirty miles into the Brokoric sea, a school of fish roasted to ash as the seven bubbles blew over them, as if a plane's exhaust had scorched them through thousands of miles of gaping sea. The knot tangled within his belly seemed infinite as the rope of his stare caught underneath the moving part of wood.

Arsena nested the side of her head in her palm as her ears turned in on the keel capering the ocean's strings.

"Semi-pleasing night," she blurted.

He bumped his elbow an inch away from hers. The scramble of letters to words from the tip of her tongue halted. "Do me a favor."

The Sifei looked over as the full moon's beam of shine dampened his soggy frown. The Pessamanti's eyes grew smokier as she grasped a hand into her trench coat pocket and snagged out a bag. The blood vessels in the Kapo's eardrums stimulated his curiosity as the sound of opening plastic laced her fingertips.

He addressed his concentration for the six loop-shaped parcels of chocolate. The Sifei's expression lightened as she chose two before she returned the bag of savory goodness to her toasty pockets.

"My dad gave this to me before he was slain, and it was rumored that he purchased these from a guard of the North-kingdom. I've never had one until now, but he instructed they should be eaten in times of extreme anguish and turmoil."

Books of wind knocked their heads at the candy. Haracle needed a lasso to pry his eyes from the buttercup-yellow lucent emitting from the center. His pulse was on a sugar high as sprinkles of yellow glitz cruised from her hand onto the hardy boards of timber.

"Want one?" she asked just as she flung the candy into the trap-door of her mouth and started chewing. Her caramel eyes were silken as the cocoa of joy moistened to chocolate milk. She stabbed her palm with the sloped angle of her middle finger as the bomb of ecstasy diffused in her belly.

Haracle skinned his hand near hers and swiped the other one. He held it inches away from his chapped lips before engaging in a minute staring contest. The right end of his ear picked up Arsena finishing whatever was left of her share with four brawny smacks.

"Mugies."

The Sifei gave Haracle a glance of her own and said, "Excuse me?"

He elevated the sweetness against his gums like a wine glass and replied, "The name of the candy is Mugies."

The invisible streak of focus from her eye sharpened in an arrow just as he launched it in his mouth like a catapult. The rapturous treat stole an ample chunk of his breath.

"Delicious, right?"

Haracle nodded.

She and the Pessamanti waited for his teeth to grind away the minor bits of delicious fudge stuck to his teeth like a sticker.

"Can I ask you a favor?" he mumbled off his tongue like a rock on a hill. She slanted the right side of her afro near his chops.

"I'm grateful for the aid you've provided so far. I know your aware of Anthony's drastic behavior. Please, out of consideration for the history we have, let me handle this."

She straightened her head and crammed the muteness with "If you say so."

The Kapos unlocked his ankles and said, "Thanks."

The umbra of her honey eyes shunned a strawberry red. Watching Haracle's body, she flapped him to the other side of the deck. She whipped her shoulders until their backs faced each other. The cinder from her boot snuck between the floor crack and cave dived on top of some sort of jail constructed of silver ore.

Seeping light through its slits of timber was the only dependable source for their eyes as his mind put him in a rooted sleep. The troll snoozing next to him missed the lake of sweat flowing from his temples to his chin. The racket of a black wooden plate stomped the table beside a pleasant carved spoon and fork. A woman rocked an identical garment as he freed a slew of stocky carrots, mushrooms, and tomatoes smothered in beef broth on his. The boy's smile appeared to be eternal as the wet curtain over her lips bonked his glabella. The kiss was brighter than the tangled flames below the cast iron pot.

He heard bubbles bursting into song as she made herself a broiling plate. His fingers folded in and around the fork like a worm before he scooped a glob of scalding stew into his mouth.

"Zestful," he deemed as the rush of vegetables and seasoned soup bounced from the roof of his crevice to the bottom like a jumping castle. He dove the utensil into the dish for another bite as the burning sensation crippled its way up his lungs and iced over his other hand. The woman in the night dress sitting in front of the teen began to shake like a still drunk. The haziness grooming his eyes exploded as he hastened them around his throat. The figure before him darkened as he hacked for the ceiling like he intended to get rid of his entire nasal cavity. The spasmed neck muscles near the boy's face slammed it along the board of wood.

He placed his palm on both ends of the table before a chili pepper tingle struck his windpipe. An epidemic of goosebumps raced for the solitary feeling from the seat of his spine. The intuition thickened as the virtuous grace leaking from her visage morphed like a card flipped left to right into a black and white tv noise. The boy's chin trembled harder than a cocktail between a bartender hands as the screech and blades of teeth drooped his cheekbones like saggy skin.

Anthony's crossed arms separated as if one was allergic to the other and gunned his head left, leaving a storm of perspiration on the row of metal bars. Anthony's scooted away about a foot more as his iris caught the beige troll indulging in a nap. He slanted his hand toward his shoulder as the troll's forehead also beamed in moisture.

"I wonder?" he whispered.

The string of saliva draped from his lower fangs like a damaged chandelier.

A ballerina of sparks danced between them in a mad clash of axe blades. General Dhanos transferred his body weight into the axe, charging for the cramped space between Captain Abornell's eyes. A cocky smirk peeked its way to the pale-eyed troll's mouth seconds before he left a bucket of air above him in a swift duck, fist bunched as the other waited diagonally across his face. The impatient twitch in his balled hands lunged for the meeting of nerves pulsating under his chin in a rippling uppercut. A cruel collision between his bark handle and his gummy soft temple dried the troll's tacky smirk.

General Dhanos's grimaced lips were iron pressed as the captain spat out a gold ball of spit before he landed on his back.

"Stand up now," the general commanded.

Captain Abornell averted his gaze before he spewed the blood hiding from under his tongue on the dullest section of his blade. The troll's feet raked his pack of bones face to face with the general. The paste color in the captain's eyes burnished when a horned pain from the ossified part of General Dhanos's elbow impaled his knee cap.

Down to one knee, the troll standing over him reminded about straying your eyes from your opponent. Another slug hijacked the letters into the apology for his right cheek before his back planted on the mat of tree bark.

The sting from his whole face couldn't take effect before another punch came crashing until the barrage obstructed his vision. The left edge of his mouth released a turbulent roar that shook through the general's assault and him out of the nightmare.

"What the!" he blabbed as he untied his bunched knuckles and mopped his hairless head. He noticed the cage he believed he had eluded from.

"How did I get back?"

"Lousy dream," Anthony commented.

A flood of adrenaline blitzed his heart.

"You!" he yelled as the nails on each hand dug two burrows into the resilient wood.

"You better plead to the seven that I don't get out again."

"Yeah, I know; you'll cleave my liver out with your teeth and stomp me until I can't be recognized. Let's fast forward past the theatrics."

Captain Abornell's grunt deflated a large sum of smoke bulging from his chest before he defrosted the iced bars with a slab of meat covering the set of his bones. He gave the troll eagle eyes.

"I'm assuming your disdain for me isn't hereditary, so there must be another reason."

Captain Abornell's belly was a couple more laughs away from tearing his gut in half.

"Does it matter?"

"What's the rush to be my enemy?"

Captain Abornell formed a ball of saliva ball from the roof of his mouth before he slung it out for the teen. The nonexistent throbbing sponge in his larynx lessened before the tire of spit bucket for the wizarding area on his cheek. The frosty light of fear glistened in his eyes as the spittle crashed into the screen of lilac lines of energy shimming between the confined bars. Anthony shook his head three times.

"When I look at you, all I see is a frail underling trying to converse ate his way out of death. If you're not going to fight me, then shut up!"

Anthony reclined against the block of lumber. He closed his eyes and reeled in his breath for eight seconds. Captain's Abornell's brain juiced in a massive head pain as the boy turned and yelled with an immersed echo, "If you wish to die by my hand, so be it."

The beige troll's bladder softened to soup while the weary bones in the lowest pressure point in his vocal cords astringed by the prick fanning from his bee- yellow iris.

"Trust me, when the times comes to bump knuckles, I'll destroy you with this eye." He grasped his fingernails in his hand before his eyes cleared to their Hershey brown. Anthony got up and walked four more feet away and sat down with his right paw of fingers gripping the center of his scalp like a basketball.

12

UNTAMED

The sun's journey finished for the day. Their heartbeat swung a homerun against their ribs as the bristles of their broom pushed the final bits of dust off the lounging broom.

A new kind of blister arose from their hands. They allowed the bottom nothingness to consume the crumbs beneath the bridge. Their chains propped at each other and they uttered "One day," as the thought of Daemok circulated through their brains. Their arms instructed their palms for one another before his torso suspended above his pal. The Brutar captive's eyes bulged in a struggle as his chest cavity poured a brew on his feet. The blood waxed on his cheek dried at the top of his lips. His thick hair stayed taped to his scalp as he sank to the bed of soil before the rock plugged his incisors.

The Brutar's fingernails stood no chance against the immeasurable force towing him backward. Busy breath in his lungs stalled as the bone connecting his upper forearm divided like a chomped sliced of meat before his left hand planted into the ground mixture like a monument. A hippogriffin prisoner varnishing the tablet of gold locked outside a goblin insignia.

"You catch an ear to that?"

The hippogriffin sloughed his concern with half a shoulder shrug. "The only thing I don't hear is your broom scrubbing those missed smudges. You know how he gets; do you want us strung up by our insides?"

Hundreds of insects crawled within his skin before he witnessed his clean-up buddy's hands sweep nothing but air as he reached for his head. He puked a waterfall in a sputter before his own escaped his fragmented skull.

The scream sailed through the Imperial doors into Daemok's ears before his eyebrows anchored over his eyeballs. A petite grin swiped between his cheeks as Imperial doors opened in a sleek squeak. A fluff of air blew open his eyelids.

"Perhaps I'll get someone to inform you on what happens If I'm kept waiting," he advised as he rose and paraded past the harrowing beast — the swiveling path of blood bathing the tiles of his marble floor. He peered at he the dead bodies and said, "Oh and you will be cleaning that up."

The train of the tunnel inside him growled as Daemok's palms vice locked stiles and shoved it shut.

A slew of miles throughout the Brokoric sea, the moon's light added an extra shine to Mr. Immel's fur coat.

Lemon eyes squeezed.

The scampering bubble bullied no sudden columns in streaks of white blurs.

Mr. Immel and laid his paws in front of his face and plodded his bent back in a perpendicular line as he clutched the roller coaster ride mangling his topside.

"I told you," Wizard Palik commented. "Last time my head pounded this bad was when I graded a test."

The wizard's proud posture limped, and he instructed the Sallus to hush for a minute. His nagging nod fur canvassed behind the flaring on his shoulders. A surprise box of silence popped seconds before he delivered his eyes forward like a pinch bar.

"Nothing; it's just we must hurry."

The Otek leader confessed as the medium winds hurling the bubbles switched to the speed of a storm.

An unseen magnet appeared to draw the flapping crow away from the Otek travelers within closer proximity of Daemok's basement. The bird gave the scientist Kulu a free art show as it crashed into the glass. He was stirring a mixture of red and purple inside a beaker with his left hand. While he walked once toward the seven bronze coffins, he scattered the vapor mix over the casket headers. The dark circles under his eyes radiated like a fluorescent bulb as the smoke cleaned itself up.

"Interesting," he mumbled before built-in heater for a neck was overwhelmed by the severe amount of ice wielded by those mysterious hands. Bright Kulu struggled for air before the loops in his iris were extracted by the chant "Su ek tu nok eveal, Conco." The hooded figure watched as Kulu's body suspended in air with his arms tucked, with enough snow in his eyes to cause a blizzard.

He strolled past him and walked back and forth before whirling his hands up and down the spiral like a fishing rod.

"Su nek extracta." The words slipped from his lips as if they were banana peels.

The wizard sipped the bolts of green energy from the coffin ike a suction cup. The last straw of aura housing within his left hand disbanded the cryptic figure. A scramble of black smoke slithered through the repressed space of the basement dormer.

The mess of starless smolder blended within the raven sky. Dawning above a ship, her trotting increased as the starving twinge waged war in her stomach. Anthony sifted the stairs with his feet, and as he climbed the steps, he clutched the rail next to him like a mature man and hauled himself onto the main deck. The mini fan gusting from Haracle's wings pulled Anthony's gaze his way like a slamming door. He stayed still as his noggin juggled whether to give him space or not. Ten undefeated minutes went by before a foot decided to go for him.

"Up ahead," sent his prime focus left at the massive structure. Anthony caught himself as he ran to the barrier of the main floor. He cocked his head as the ship's paws leaned them within the islet's reach. The teen must have had guns for eyebrows, the way they shot up at the Brutar ghost who appeared beside him in the pad of smoke.

"I wish I could say it's a pleasure but get ready."

Anthony returned his stare to the bathing trunk of land smothered in trees and rock.

"Tremor Island," Sir Fowke mumbled with a toxic pout as the ship drifted for the colossal unknown.

13

BRAWL

Rockets of air failed to dodge the shingles thrashing from the dragon's armor as he sailed above the Pegleg forest. Amazement appeared near his scarred eye as the plane of dense energy belly-danced some yards from him.

General Ino's rainbow beak added an extra coated sleek to the blackish coat of the snake general as it glided through dank soil.

General Byron squinted up at the pipe of wind plumbing above his lethal head.

"Brothers up ahead."

A polluted red castle pried its way into view. The two other general's wide eyes thinned out as the dragon in silver wings collected another funnel of air and spun like a bullet for the fort hold of interest.

The horn he had for a goatee swayed his mouth as a flurry of scratches rained on the back of his head. General Ton screamed in a runnel of fire as the sprite of gore ran over his armored face like strawberry syrup. The serpent general slithered, abandoning a trail of sparks as he raced next to his brother.

"You alright, brother?"

General Ton shook the party of blood on his armor off and let his brothers know he was fine, and to stay watchful. Generals Inc and Byron dug his serpent body more in-depth into the humic dirt below slicing metal.

They scanned the vacant space of water and mud as secrecy filled their abstaining ears. A hammer of blows struck the top of the snake's head until his reptilian eyeballs nearly juiced out of his skull.

"Brother Byron!" the dragon yelled before his wings dragged through the pavement of soil with brisk force. The oversized snake chased the shrill opera clanging from his armor. The slick kente pattern on his neck minded with each coiled strike into a pouch of air. The spacious gap between his fangs caught two portions of tree bark.

General Ino clawed scoops of wind, daring to puncture the entity carting the dragon general like a tow truck. The pink scar color of his eye dulled as the side of the snake's torso came together as if he was caught inside a contraption of gears.

"No," shot out their lungs and ripped a tear into the night skies. The snake's two front teeth clobbered into the turf. He raked the dirt as he found himself trekking from his brothers like a tempered child.

The hippogriffin used every muscle in his wings to launch himself forward; halfway through the boost, an invisible comet lit his whole body on fire. General Ton cried, as he could do nothing but watch as the tango of fire grew smaller until the bird disintegrated to charcoal bits.

General Ton slung his shoulders and spun his head like a compact disc while tearing out a new vocal cord, releasing rings of fire. His wings hovered above the pools of fire. The right eye struggled left and right, expecting any sign of General Byron through the fuzzy hotness. The longer he stood flapping above the ember mess, he made it a lot easier for the sterling armor to soften into his flesh.

Stings all over his neck broke him out of the trance before he made off from the area with a single wing. As he was flying like a crazy drunk farther away, an immersed grumble boiled out of his breadbasket. Tuzank's nests nipped in a pom of sticks as the howl burped the oracular being out of the way and miles into the glass window within the tawny bars of the enclosure. She hurled her blade of nails in and out the tummies of Sifei and Sallus.

The blood witch responsible smudged a bowl of blood on her onyx-colored nails to soothe jarred butterflies playing in her tummy. She leveled the pleats from the back of her robe with a dire some amount of organ fluid. She then directed her arms up and down in a puddle of death like a little kid playing in the snow for the first time. The woman slumbering within the jail of gold shot up from another hair-stiffening ordeal.

Gagging on gulps of her saliva, she accidentally swallowed a tarty spoonful.

"Anthony," she whispered.

Candis would have assumed she wet the cardinal pillow under her bum if she had not taken notice of the perspiration lake flowing out of every pore. The open cage door squeaking back and forth snatched her eyeballs. Her available glare ignored her feet, as she took a foot out of the cage one after the other on the floor. She tiptoed through and out of the goblin's king's bedchambers for the Imperial hall. She pressed them against the right side of the door with her left palm. The edge of her mouth downturned as her eyes sniped the humongous glass window behind a greasy chair of gold, he called a throne.

The sounds of her footsteps stopped in front of the window. Whips struck the infant air as hundreds of stones were lifted and banged into. The consistent breath traveling out of her lungs went shallow just as a slave below revealed a stubby quantity of lashes on a Brutar royal's back.

"Does this displease you?" the ant-crawling voice asked behind her.

Candis's head followed the downward shrug of her collarbones.

"Bastard."

The goblin king tipped his chin upward in length and replied, "Careful, or I might start believing that's my name." He returned the bottom half of his face straight ahead. "I'm surprised the sight of this is bothersome, especially to someone like you." The inside of her eyes exploded mentally as Daemok leaned for the middle of his ear.

"I know what you are."

Candis shifted side to side like a thermostat lever. The red imprint from her open hand against his cheek faded like a body heat device after it's been touched.

"You know nothing," she claimed.

He brushed off her vicious slap with the flicker of his outside hand as he waffle-pressed his behind on his throne. "Trust that it pains me more to see you in this flawed state."

Anthony's mother twisted herself away from the brutal labored captives below.

"Why the sudden broken lock?"

"Would you believe me if said I am working on my trust issues?"

He continued to lurk at her shaking her head. "You'll never have to worry about suffering the same fate," he exclaimed.

"And If I want to?" she inquired.

"Do you?"

She disregarded his reply and moved from within the window's grasp. He smirked as she walked past and away from him.

"One last thing," he blurted.

"You're no prisoner in the castle, but outside of that, who knows?"

She stopped at the door as if a playful block stood in her way. The goblin king observed as she weaseled her chocolate body through the threadlike space outside of the Imperial doors.

The pleasant clangs of metal slapping one another in his head drooped. The clanging sparkled louder than his spear end. The green hand coiled around the weapon's guard aimed for a set of Brutar legs below. The hooves jumped above the cleaved spear before he thumped a brand into his upper body. The goblin whisked toward the ground in a backward roll. The tips of his five toes rounded up a shovel of dirt before he propelled forward with white teeth for the Brutar knight. He bobbed with his knees bent as the blade sliced a cleft of hair below his ducked head.

The goblin king countered his breath as his spear guard swept the goblin's ankles into the air. The Brutar knight tucked his spear by his side as the beryl-green plat of the goblin's skin swathed over his back onto the box of soot. He walked up to the goblin warrior lying in a cushion of grass and offered him his right hand.

"On your feet. warrior."

The goblin wobbled his head left and right before he clamped his right hand on the Brutar's welcoming left. He lobbed his other hand over his shoulders and warned him about watching his left side.

"Yeah, yeah," he answered.

Fenced between trees, the Brutar knight kept his arms leaned over his collar bone as the pads of wood over their knees and elbows were transported toward mammoth pillars in size holding up an enormous emerald castle. The corners of their lips stretched into a grin as their eyes chucked a stream of joyous light at the enchanting palace.

"Gets more gorgeous every time I see it," he asserted.

"With our tiresome training and studies, we shall ensure peace and fairness throughout Chaizo."

The Brutar knight's brain fizzled like fresh soda as another Brutar--shorter than him, with a crown just as green as the castle--paraded her appearance. The blue, red, and yellow jewels circling her crown abandoned the goblin's mind in one thought.

"That's some impressive display of stonework."

The face of the goblin by his side lit up like a stain on a white shirt as the goblin next to her tugged the sides of her dress before he followed the Brutar queen past the guards into the castle's entrance.

"Now's your chance to talk to her," he expressed just as the knight's iris caught itself in a fishnet stare. He unclenched his fists as the camera in his eyes spat out the flashback onto the goblin king's lap.

14

CAPTIVATED

A summit of damp sand invited the ship the ship ashore. Sir Fowke released the string of detaining the piece of walking board. A yoga ball of dust struck from the slamming strip of wood. The orb of Anthony's soles was first to roam down and off the ship. He smuggled his concentration for the sky-tickling palm trees posing around him. Arsena's attention span was short-lived as she moved her black pelted bundle behind the boy.

"I've only heard of this in my uncle's journal."

Her Pitbull of smoke scanned the perimeter of sand and trees as Benevlo's crimson toes scuffed a butte of sand. Sir Fowke studied the black hole, drawing his eyes into the forest front of him.

"It would be wise to settle in for the night before starting our misguided tour."

"If you insist," Anthony responded with a tuned-out voice.

A surge of wind showed him off the boat within the bounds of heat bloating forth his fur. He sat across in front of fire Anthony with his head sideways. The teen returned the favor as the Sifei's hand steady hand collapsed over her stomach as if she wanted to hide her fat.

"What do you suppose we'll run into?" he asked.

Sir Fowke shrugged his question off like a dust mop. During their conversation, Anthony sat up and took a couple of steps over to Haracle. He kneeled beside him and let out a tiny breeze from his mouth. "Hey man, I know I've--" The teen couldn't finish his sentence.

"Save it, because honestly, I'm reaching the point where I couldn't care less."

The color in his eyes was washed out. He stood back up and re-treated to his seat before the boot print stranded in the sand stole his fixation. Haracle stored his focus within the barriers of fire as the words of debate ditched their lips while Anthony crept forward within the black abyss of clumpy saplings.

Miles into the clutter of strange, the pace of boots slowed at a turtle's rate. Her back was bent as if she was carrying a mountain on top before she scraped her palm against a tree trunk. She wheezed like an exhausted cheetah before an odor satisfied her famished nostrils. She raised her head in a distant mile as her eyes stabbed the hip of the Dyra, inhaling packets of leaves.

Arsena's iris flashed between caramel brown and a sapped red. She gazed at the deer glistening with diamond skin and thought one word: meat. She radiated her stare side to side like a pair of open and closed scissors. The hunger-crazed teenager concealed the roof of her back foot on into the terrain before she sent a tomb of sand flying as she charged for the Dyra. Deeper in the route of gore drops, step after step the desert in his throat became even dryer. The teen unhooked his posture as the pinches of blood trailed into a sickening pond.

Anthony's bottom lip curled while fighting to deflect his gaze from the mutilated buck. Silverfish loops of the beast's liver and kidneys spilled from her fangs. In his mind, he raced his hands over his jaws as Arsena slapped her back against the tree's stalk behind her. She anchored her head at chin level, stained with blood below, shaking in a hail of tears.

"Help me," she pleaded.

Anthony picked his FRO hawk with all ten fingers as he rambled past the miserable teenage girl and farther into the wall of trees. His top and lower teeth bullied one another as one more set of eight flashes of film developed a black goblin sitting on his throne with a lady behind appeared to much like his mother in his brain. A flickering flashlight showcased from his eyes.

Anthony's stride ramped up the deeper he trotted into a full-blown sprint. Another foot or two before a grimacing tune itched his busy legs to sleep. The two corners on his forehead oozed in excessive secretion.

"Kre nak, nu see no tu" played like a scuffed vinyl.

He indulged in a more in-depth glance at the creatures responsible. He counted a party of Kranaks, Sallus Nairy rolling around a spilt tree trunk quenched in a fire. A Kranak's feather jolted up like a standing knife as the distraught teen strained itself in his view. The other beings of song proceeded by his head.

"You look unwell," a Kranak commented.

"Maybe you have a drink? We have plenty."

Anthony put his head of bones down as the canary-yellow titter in his iris overwhelmed his almond browns.

"Run," fled his mouth.

The Sallus's eyebrows above his furry head cupped as she asked, "What did you?"

Anthony gave him no time to digest the rest of his sentence before a massive spelled grenade in his porch belly whooshed to pieces like an exploding cherry pie.

Cries of uplifting song fell victim to a high-pitched holler as half the gathered circle flinched in front of a wand of air caped around their throats. The sinister presence revealed the boy's row of teeth, while the wind collared on their necks cuddled in a trachea-crushing grip.

The yellow gleamed in his eyes like a streetlight as it seized at the last four creatures stumbling beside each other in a precise two hundred and eighty steps. He hiked his head in a knife position and chopped it horizontally for the heart-jumped individuals. It was as if two ropes were on both sides of his mouth drawing from the other half a second before a shank of wind separated their torsos from their waist. The axed breeze cut through an entire palm tree before being devoured into sugary ash.

The make-out session between the tree base and the sancy floor stopped as the jammed sparkle in his eyes fought to remain lit like a shooting star about to disappear. The pinball ricocheted all crooks in his brain and weakened his kneecaps on the forest boards. Two shadows faced and hurled "Conco!"

The chant bulged the boy's eyes at the side of his sockets before his drapery eyebrows tapped them back into place. A team of shadows preserved their stares as the teen lay flat out on his belly saturated in a layer of blood. Haracle flapped his way next to the Brutar ghost and crimson troll before his head winded to the side as the lagoon of red bubbles from the carnage finished.

15

RAPTURE

Queen Kedar nibbled on her talons while the others traded words of gossip.

"Then it's agreed."

Sir Canshu's eyes played tennis with the queen's hand moving back and forth over a blooming sunflower. The sliver of chat from the Imperial hall washed above his ears.

"She's not in her right mind to make my decision."

"You can't blame her," Queen Abbassi stated. The snake queen combed the bottom of her scales in a tight slither.

"Of course, we do not."

"Save it," Sir Canshu interrupted.

The queen of dragons could sense the blood sprinting through Queen Kedar's head.

"This is royal business and no concern of yours."

The side of his jaw cramped in a stew of gossip ready to be released.

"Help!" came as loud as the damaged wing bringing him to a Goliath-sized door. The four dashed their way out of the Imperial hall. The entryway couldn't finish opening before "General Ton" abandoned his lips.

He galloped a little closer before the metallic workshop of armor cushioned his body from the granite steps. Blood spewed from his mouth like an overflowing cup.

"General, what happened?" the Brutar asked.

He coughed up three more balls of gore and responded, "We were ambushed."

The needles of hair he possessed for eyebrows knitted themselves.

"By who?"

"Not who, but what." The feeling of ten fists beating from inside his ribcage to get out hindered his muscles as the dragon general's shutters blinked him to sleep. A nest of Tuzanks swarmed in a hurricane formation in front of the fortress entrance. A frail sheer of sweat wandered beneath his nose as he stood up. He shot his right hand at the queens behind him and told them to stay here and tend to the general's wounds.

The three held a get-together with their eyes for the stained blood decorated on his armor. The Brutar knight galloped for the doorway. He flattened his look against eight sets of ruby bricks.

Eight, seven, six...they severed apart like dwindling blocks. The Brutar queen huffed her breathing under control next to Sir Canshu as her eyeballs sprang for the circles her protector wafted.

"What is it?" she asked.

She replicated his head direction and darted her pair of lookers at the legion of beguiled beings--Kranaks, Sukaats, dragons, serpents, and more.

"We require aid."

"Is there any more room?"

Sir Canshu slung the surface of his skull a hair away from his queen's cheek before she returned his interest with a head shifted into his path. The oven around her heart smelted away the ice valves as the noticeable number of coughs from children mobbed her ears.

"Let them in."

The nighty ovals beside his eyes darkened and countered, "My queen, I'm not sure that is wise."

He moved his chin side to side like a biometric scanner.

"Should we at least discuss this with the others?"

She exhaled the tube of stress constructing her lungs.

"If that's what you want," he answered and took an exact ten back. The jam-packed forest cleaned itself out as the survivors entered the fortress. Queen Merrick seemed like she forgot how to count as numerous "thank you's" were sent her way. The eight sets of bricks began to confine the bridge of space on which they came. Sir Canshu let out a covert chuckle as the clear bulbs in their eyes brightened.

He walked with his fingers locked behind his back next to his queen. Their eyebrows arched as hundreds of beings filled the shore of space.

"I hope you're right," the Brutar knight uttered.

The case of Tuzaaks fled twenty miles from the area above and over the protected chain.

"Move it!" Reznark's breathing outran at him every turn. The links tightened the shale around his hands at each tug. The goblin with the Dyra skull inclined across his face stole his last steps up the hill. The broils stuck to his face each second as he kept his eyes on the castle smeared in black. The set of seventy goblins behind him drummed their feet. Chulko trucked the Dyra skull over his face and replied, "Chums were home."

The percussion set performing shook the most entrenched grass in a dance as they marched forward.

16

PECULIAR

A litter of clay in goblin form shattering to doughy rumble broke the boy of out of the illusion. Rocking, the light in his eyes intensified as it added to the shine of the prison bars of shackles around him.

"Make way," the voice in front of him requested.

The beast had large pointy ears and was six hairs away from being bald. He wasn't the only one the boy observed; the chocolate within his pupils glossed over the town of beasts who took the same appearance. Kicking sand as the teen cruised through the city of palm tree, a shale-hooded woman darker than the hair on Arsena's scalp fanned her right hand over her breastbone after the she walked past her in chains.

Three minutes skimmed by before the women curved her head to the left for a man who also fashioned a slouchy hood. Up and down her chin went before he dispersed faster than she could blink.

She retreated her stare back at the Sifei in bondage as the corner of her right eye held on to the caged boy. Anthony shook his hands and legs, expecting five, before the hollowness in his chest gave them meaningless air like Sir Fowke's presence within the fiasco.

"Come on," rushed from his lips as he tried again.

The teen's knuckles cracked his own as his drowsy gawk hocked into the chain of string around the Kapos's mouth and wings. The man with the hood smiled at Anthony's back before he shadow-dashed beside a bat-looking beast and left the sweet word smack on the back of his head.

The creature rubbed the rear end of his head as his nostrils flared a factory of smoke. He howled a mitted hand to the person next to him.

"Serves you more than right."

The victim of his punch massaged his cheek and returned the act of violence. A half an hour couldn't have slept before the left side of the cleared path stood blindly in kicks and punches.

Arsena swished her wrist within the restraint as her shoulder and wrist tingled a salient sting before her back met the teensy pellets on the ground. The woman with the hood cuffed her hand on Arsena's mouth.

"Don't talk, listen. You understand?" She bowed her head like a person with no neck bones.

The woman rushed her eyes forward before proving her resonate shadow dash within the combative crowd. Anthony's visage molded in concentration as the creature treading his entrapment hauled his metallic jail within range of the boundless spiral corroded into the rock above the concerned space.

The green fire rupturing from his left hand like a young match illuminated his whole face like a dark tunnel.

"Anthony is it?" he said with his cheekbones striving for the crannies of his forehead before it let go an inestimable volume of pressured laughter. The goblin king's explosion of chuckles swam like a tidal wave through the Pegleg Forest over the Brokoric Sea and died on the herniated crack crumbing from the spiral of stone. The row of bat- appearing beings held captive inside a suede leather of armor strapped to their legs and chest grew duskier in feeling like the boy's cage. Anthony's eyes pinched like salt as the light from outside faded. The bracelet of glowing red from their iris fought the pitch dark. Thirty more steps he counted before the cage wrangling side to side came to a stop. The boy's eyes arched as the jail box kissed the ground. Silence drowned the cave like a running faucet. The stance in the boy's heart pumped offbeat to unshackling metal.

"Touch me again, and you'll never be too."

They ignored the boy's tantrum and kept his wrist locked in their hands. Anthony's eyes and cheeks turned hot as his back met the gravel from the callous terrain. The teen's posture and focus were brought back on his feet above the bully of rock.

Haracle's ears perked as the boy's shirt was ripped in a hymn. Its nails dug a banquet into his shoulder blades. A sour case of air briefed under his tongue as his kneecaps tackled the portrait of stones. A beehive of pricks beat his knees as the bat creature grabbed a shady iron rod behind his back. Anthony's iris scrambled like bad eggs as Haracle's body pitched ten feet from his bowing friend. He sneaked his hand into his pocket and grabbed his sun dial.

10:00 on the dot, he thought before he veered toward a twitching orange shine burning from the rod. Anthony bunched his hands as the laminating heat stroked his right pec.

The summer of Anthony's pride kept his awareness deadbolted on the creature's vermillion peepers as the lava hot pole merged into his flesh. The boy rinsed the parched rocks below in sweat. Tight grunts of his pal accompanied the loneliness in the Kapcs's ears.

"Even though I'm still pissed, it still would be difficult for me not to wish you a happy sixteenth birthday."

The Kapos's hums were undetected like a ninja as the other noise of Anthony's squawks echoed throughout the cave of Tremor Island.

17

WELCOME

"Get those backs moving."

The abrupt hollow in his whip slashed the air harder than the tips of their hammers.

The goblin with the belt eyes lagged for a Sifei who let go of the tool blistering her palm, toward a jumping bean of rocks. A Brutar with a black collar twined around his neck watched as the stones hopped higher with each step. A power box of electricity surged through every vein with urgency as the legion of green bellies above their feet walked over the hill.

The sentinel goblin belly flapped his way down the jagged stone he stood on.

"Irreparable," he whispered.

The relaxed pressure in his blood leaped as his eyes stalked the fleet of goblins cross the granite bridge behind one sporting a Dyra skull over his face. His eyebrows burrowed together toward the lack of motion from the captives and shouted, "Back to work," as she sauntered over to the entrance.

The lambent seal from the castle's door freed itself through the cracks as they opened.

Sir Gitteex arose from the exposed shutters first in a five-second stand before he took another step to his right. The outer corner of maroon in his eye blushed down the black sheet cradling the sleek patterned maze of gold above it.

"They're here, my lord," Sir Gitteex confirmed.

Daemok's speaking box stayed closed as it stopped three feet in front of them.

The goblin king's feet hugged the marble tiles below as the tank of creatures with a similar scary appearance marched closer to his direction. Chulko sailed his arm above his head. They halted behind him as he raised the buck's cerebrum in bone form to the top of his. The goblin in black and many green lips fastened in a clear-cut curl before the quiet stripped the surrounding area of their voices. An abusive candle of wind pried them to reveal their hostages of teeth.

Their hands stretched for each other's before they slapped it twice on the opposite ends concluding to an L formation with their arms over their heads.

"It's good to see you, my lord."

The goblin king shot his other up and said, "No, you call me brother, for that's what you have been to me all along."

Chulko's teeth grated half a sneer as Daemok's right hand glided for the destitute space within the door's frame.

www.ingramcontent.com/pod-product-compliance
Lightning Source LLC
Chambersburg PA
CBHW032152020726
47496CB00003B/843